# Kirall's Kiss

∞ ∞ ∞ ∞ ∞

M.K. Eidem

M.K. EIDEM

# The Imperial Series

Cassandra's Challenge

Victoria's Challenge

Jacinda's Challenge

# Tornians

Grim

A Grim Holiday

Wray

Oryon

Ynyr

# Kaliszians

Nikhil

Published by M.K. Eidem

Copyright © 2016 by Michelle K. Eidem

Cover Design by Judy Bullard

Edited by: www.A-Z_Media@outlook.com

∞ ∞ ∞ ∞ ∞

I want to thank my family for all their support. I would also like to thank all those that have been there to answer questions and help guide me; Reece, Julie, Sally Fern, Beth, Narelle and my sister Annie, thanks Ladies!

∞ ∞ ∞ ∞ ∞

# Chapter One

The Dragon's enraged roar filled the air, his wingspan casting a large shadow on the land below. His prey became nothing more than a speck as the ship it was on escaped the planet's atmosphere. With one last roar of challenge that the Dragon knew General Terron would never accept, he turned and surveyed the battleground below; bodies littered it. Some were Terceirians, the species the Dragon was fighting with and for, but the majority of them were Varanian soldiers left behind as their leader fled.

They had finally been victorious over the invading horde of Varana, but the cost had been high. The decimated planet, Terceira, and its inhabitants were nearly wiped out before enough help had arrived in the form of two Dragoons, and ships filled with the fiercest fighters from every corner of the universe.

Still General Terron had been able to escape.

That infuriated the Dragon because it meant they'd have to go through all this again when Terron attacked another planet whose inhabitants were weaker than him. The Dragon nearly had Terron, but the General slipped away when Dafydd, the leader of the Terceirians, was surrounded by five Varana. The short amount of time it took him to save Dafydd had allowed Terron to escape.

As his large, clawed feet touched the ground, the Dragon shifted into what was known as his Battle Beast form, a different kind of killing machine; one that stood on two legs and worked better in tight quarters. His Battle Beast also didn't kill *everyone* in its path, just the enemy.

"Terron got away," Dafydd walked up to the Beast, his eyes looking to the sky. "You should not have come to my aid, Kirall."

"Your people wouldn't have survived without you, Dafydd," the Beast growled. "I will kill the General another day."

"But until then, others will suffer as my people have," Dafydd sighed heavily.

"If that is Kur's will."

∞ ∞ ∞ ∞ ∞

Dacke found himself slammed down onto his back for a third time, and this time he wheezed as he tried to catch his breath.

"Kur, Kirall! What are you trying to do?" he wheezed. "Kill me? We're supposed to be sparring! You are attacking like I'm General Terron!"

Kirall forced himself to take a step away from his friend. Dacke was a Minor Dragoon, and therefore smaller and weaker than him, no matter his color. What was wrong with him? Dacke was right. He was attacking as if he wanted to kill. It had been a month since they'd vanquished the Varana from Terceira. While he didn't like staying in his Other form for so long, it was necessary when traveling in space. If he didn't, his Battle Beast would rampage, and his Dragon... well, there was no ship large enough to contain a Prime Dragoon in his Dragon form.

The ship they were currently on, the Inferno, was returning them to their home on Mondu. The Inferno was out patrolling this distant part of the universe when they received the Terceirians call for help. It wasn't until they arrived on Terceira that anyone realized just how dire the situation really was. The Varana were launching a full out assault on Terceira, and had already killed half the planet's inhabitants. Dacke immediately requested that another Dragoon be sent to assist him, and Kirall volunteered to assist his friend.

Spinning on his heel, Kirall moved to stare out the observation window of the Inferno. Before returning home, they were stopping at the small planet he could see growing larger in the distance. Some of the males wished to spend some recreation time with the local females.

Kirall was getting his first look at this small planet and its moon, since the ship he had taken to Terceira had used a more direct route. Dacke and this ship stopped at this planet nearly a year ago. All Dacke could talk about was how he couldn't wait to experience the female he met a year ago again.

Kristy.

Every male on the ship had been regaled with stories of her willingness to not only produce loud sounds, but to use all her orifices. He had requested she be invited back to the 'gathering' as they called it, and had been informed she had accepted. He was the envy of every male on the ship.

Kirall stared at the planet's moon, and as he did he felt it pull at him, filling him with a strange need. A full body shudder went through his massive frame, and he looked down in shock to see his claws digging into the metal rail he was gripping, and heard his Dragon hiss loudly in his head.

No! This couldn't be happening. Not here! Not now!

"Kirall..." Dacke approached cautiously. Even though he and Kirall had been friends for hundreds of years, he had never seen him like this before. Kirall was a Prime Dragoon, a Black, the strongest and most powerful of their kind. He could easily destroy Dacke if he wanted to. "Is there a problem?"

"Kur, yes!" Kirall spun around, and his elongating eyes had Dacke taking a startled step back. "I'm starting my Joining Heat!"

"What?!! Here?!! But... is it..."

"No! It's only been forty-six years since my last heat." They both knew a Dragoon only went into a Joining heat every hundred years.

"How is it possible then?" Dacke demanded.

"I don't know, but the closer we get to this planet's moon, the stronger it gets!"

"Then I offer you Kristy," Dacke immediately told him even though his own Dragon roared in protest.

"What?" Kirall looked at him in shock, knowing how much Dacke had been anticipating being with this female again.

"Kristy is a very accommodating female. She will enthusiastically respond to all your needs, and as I have said, she is very willing to give you her sounds of pleasure. You will need that during this Heat."

"She was to be yours," Kirall said.

"I know, but we both know what will happen if you reach your full heat before you find a willing female."

"My Beast will rampage."

"And take any female available until he finds one that satisfies him."

Kirall sighed heavily because he knew Dacke's words were true. It was why a male Dragoon always made careful preparation for his oncoming heat. A heat he should have known was coming for months, not mere hours. Why was this one so different? He wished he could contact his father and ask.

"Thank you, my friend. I accept the use of your Kristy. When we return to Mondu, I will find a way to repay you."

"Not killing me during sparring is payment enough." Dacke smiled, moving back into a sparring position, not wanting Kirall to know how truly concerned he was. A planet's moon shouldn't be able to trigger a Dragoon's Joining Heat. He needed to speak to the Healer as soon as possible. "Ready?"

Kirall moved to stand in front of Dacke assuming a sparring position. He knew what his friend was doing, and could also see the concern he was trying to hide. Only extremely old Dragoons experienced sudden Joining Heats. It was because they never found their mates, and were losing control of their Dragon. Those Dragoons were eventually ended because they were a threat to all females.

That couldn't be what was happening to him. He was only four hundred and forty-six years old. He had millennia before he had to worry about that.

"Begin!" Kirall ordered, and both males moved.

∞ ∞ ∞ ∞ ∞

"This is never going to work, Kristy," Autumn said for the umpteenth time. Autumn watched in the mirror as Kristy attempted to tame Autumn's unruly hair, and make it look like her own.

"It will," Kristy huffed out. "How can you stand to have hair like this? You need to go to a stylist, and have them do something with it. Especially these ends."

Kristy lifted some of the hair that so offended her. She'd never seen anything like the shimmery white that appeared along the last two inches of Autumn's amazing red hair. It was what had first caught her attention when she'd seen Autumn waitressing in the diner down the street from her apartment. When the light struck the ends just right, they almost looked silver, and Kristy was always looking for a way to make herself stand out. So she struck up a conversation with the waitress. Something she normally never would have done because... well... the girl really wasn't up to Kristy's standards. But she had to know about the tips, and also how she'd managed to get those perfect shades of bright, medium, and dark red in her hair. That stylist was money.

She hadn't believed Autumn when she said it was all natural. Kristy had been spending a fortune trying to achieve that exact color, and for this girl to have had it all her life and done *nothing* to earn it? That wasn't fair. So Kristy made it her mission to earn the waitress' trust, something that was harder than she had expected, hoping to find out the truth.

That had been three months ago. Two months ago, she'd convinced Autumn to move in with her, giving her a crazy low price to rent out her spare bedroom. It hadn't taken her long to realize that Autumn was telling her the truth, since it was nearly impossible to keep secrets from roommates. Autumn had no special hair products, made no appointments at salons, and the girl's wardrobe....

No, Autumn had been telling her the truth. Her amazing hair was natural and because of that, Kristy planned on telling her she had to move out. Anyone that came by her apartment seemed more interested in Autumn than in Kristy, and that just wouldn't do.

Then this little problem had come up.

A year ago, Kristy had been invited to a swanky party to serve rich, out-of-town men looking for a good time. Kristy had just ditched her boyfriend, and as she was always up for a good party and good sex, she'd willingly gone. It wasn't until she'd arrived that she discovered they actually expected her to 'serve' the men. As in drinks. As if *she* was a waitress.

It hadn't taken long for one of the men to single her out. He'd been tall, good-looking... She frowned, trying to remember more about him and found her mind blank. That was strange. She must have drunk too much. But she knew she'd had sex, and a lot of it, because when she'd gotten home her body had been sore in ways only sex could cause, *and* they'd paid her ten grand.

A month ago, right before Autumn had moved in, she'd received a call from a Mr. Bonn, telling her that Mr. Dacke would be returning, and that he had requested she be there. Kristy had pretended disinterest at first, but when this Bonn guy had told her they would pay her twenty grand with a two thousand dollar advance, she'd readily agreed.

Things had changed in the last month. Kristy had started dating a very wealthy guy who treated her like a princess, showering her with gifts, and taking her on exotic trips. She wasn't going to screw that up for a paltry twenty thousand dollars.

But someone had to go since she'd already spent the two thousand dollars, and that's where Autumn came in. If she could just get Autumn's hair to cooperate then there was a good chance Autumn could pass for Kristy. She felt a little twinge of guilt because she was pretty sure Autumn was a virgin, but she ignored it. Who in this day and age was still a virgin at the age of twenty-two? She would be doing Autumn a favor, getting her laid, plus she'd told Autumn she could have the remaining money she had been promised.... Well, not all the money.

Kristy wasn't stupid, after all. This was only happening because of *her,* so she deserved a share of the money. She had cried, ruining her makeup, as she convinced Autumn to take her place; telling her she would lose Philip if she went, and would be in big trouble if she didn't. She'd sworn that all

Autumn had to do was serve drinks, just like she did at her night job, only this one paid a lot more.

Autumn had been skeptical because they both knew Kristy didn't 'wait' on anyone. But Kristy had quickly spun a tale about how the boyfriend she'd had, before the two of them met, had cleared out her bank account. She'd been desperate for money until it had gotten sorted out. Autumn seemed to believe that, silly girl. Like Kristy would ever let a man get the better of her.

She'd then gone on to tell Autumn that the remaining eight thousand would be hers, and then Autumn could take the night classes she'd been talking about... and find her own apartment. Not that Kristy had said *that*.

So here she was, doing her best to get the shorter, thinner Autumn to look like her. And yes, she hated Autumn for that. All of this, so Kristy could go away with Philip for a weekend trip to his private island in the Caribbean.

∞ ∞ ∞ ∞ ∞

Autumn sat in the back of the limo. She couldn't believe she had agreed to this. Something didn't ring true in the story Kristy had told her. Even if Kristy had been broke, Autumn couldn't see her serving drinks to out-of-towners, wealthy or not. Autumn did that at her night job, and they *always* expected more for their tips than just drinks. But eight thousand dollars for two nights work.... She couldn't pass that up. It would change her life.

The limo slowing down pulled her from her thoughts, just in time to see them enter an underground garage.

Where was she? She should have been paying closer attention to where they were taking her; instead she'd been lost in thought.

When the door of the limo opened, Autumn slid out, not very gracefully. She stood, clenching the purse that held the copy of Kristy's I.D. and paperwork.

"You Kristy Pwff?" A big man, with a face only a mother could love, asked.

"Yes." She handed him the papers.

"Follow me," he ordered taking the paperwork from her without even glancing at it. He led her past a line of women who were all different shapes and sizes, then down a hallway. Were those the women she would be working with? She never got to ask when her escort opened a door and gestured her inside.

No one noticed the large figure lurking in the shadows.

"Kristy Pwff," he announced to another even bigger man.

"Kristy, I'm not sure if you remember me." He took the paperwork, tossing it on the table behind him. For some reason, the man behind her snickered as if they were sharing a private joke. "I'm Mr. Bonn. I'm the one that contacted you on behalf of Mr. Dacke."

"Mr. Bonn," Autumn nodded slightly, but didn't smile. She'd met his kind before. The kind who believed that because they were big and strong they had the right to prey on those smaller and weaker than them. The kind that enjoyed doing it. If the men at this party were like him, she was in big trouble.

"You can put your clothes in one of those lockers. Here's your uniform." He shoved a hanger at her.

Autumn barely contained her gasp as she looked at what little fabric there was on the hanger.

"I'll be back in ten minutes, and we'll get you to where you are needed." With that, Bonn and the other man exited the room through a different door.

Autumn stared at the door, her unease growing. Walking back to the door she'd entered, she discovered there was no inside handle. There was only going to be one way out of this room, and she was sure it would only be allowed if she changed. Looking at the clock on the wall, she saw she was down to six minutes. Keeping one eye on the door, she stripped down to her bra and panties. There was no way she was giving those up. Quickly she put on the tiny top and skirt they'd given her. She knew the scars on her back would be easily seen through the sheer fabric of the top, but there was nothing she could do about that. She'd barely finished buttoning up the shirt when Bonn reentered the room. The way his eyes ran over her exposed skin had her shivering in revulsion.

Bonn let his eyes travel over the woman that he'd had to put so much effort into getting here, and didn't understand what the fuss was all about. She wasn't much to look at, as far as he was concerned. He liked his women with big boobs and little brains. This one looked just the opposite, as her eyes assessed him.

"Here, take this." Bonn held out a small, clear container that held a white pill.

"What's that?" Autumn immediately asked, making no move to take it.

"It's an energy pill. You'll need it for what you're going to be doing."

"I'll be fine without it," she told him.

"You will take it." Bonn took a menacing step toward her. "Or I will make you take it."

Autumn saw he meant it, and did the only thing she could. She reached out and took the container. "I'll need some water." She didn't, but Bonn didn't know that.

"Take the pill, and I'll get you some," he ordered, his eyes narrowing.

Autumn raised the container to her mouth, tipped her head back tossing the pill in, and swallowed before handing the container back to him.

"Open your mouth," he ordered.

Autumn knew he was going to demand that, and immediately opened her mouth showing him it was empty.

"Water," she demanded, refusing to give him the upper hand. With a grunt, he went to the minifridge she hadn't seen before, and as he did, she spit out the pill she'd hidden under her tongue.

"Here." He thrust a bottle at her. "Drink then you need to get to work."

# Chapter Two

Kirall was enraged. He couldn't believe this was happening to him.

To him.

A Prime Dragoon.

One of the most powerful of his kind.

He controlled his Beast. His Beast didn't control him. But today it seemed it did.

Rising from the couch, he went and poured himself a drink of what they called Fire Water on this planet.

Fire Water.

Really?

They had to be joking. A female Dragoon gave their young nourishment that was stronger than this. Tossing the drink back, he returned to the couch.

He needed Kristy to arrive, and soon. His Beast was close to the surface, demanding to be released.

He'd tried to contact his father before he had to travel to the surface, but with the great distance between this planet and Mondu, he had yet to receive a response when he needed to leave the Inferno.

A Dragoon was only supposed to go into a Joining Heat once every hundred years. He didn't understand why his had been triggered so soon.

He hoped this Kristy was as willing with her body and sounds as Dacke had claimed, because he was going to need it. Already the anticipation of those things had Kirall's cock swelling, and he ripped open his pants to ease the pressure. Flinging his arms out, his claws dug into the back of the couch as another wave of Heat hit, causing his hips to arch up in need.

If the female didn't arrive soon, he would be unable to control his Beast.

Just as the thought crossed his mind, the door to his temporary rooms opened.

∞ ∞ ∞ ∞ ∞

Entering the room Bonn had led her to, Autumn began to wonder just what the hell Kristy had gotten her into. Obviously she'd been totally lied to. Why Autumn was surprised, she didn't know. She'd always known Kristy wanted something from her. She'd just never been able to figure out what it was, and a small part of her had hoped they would become friends. She'd been wrong.

Now she just needed to figure out how to get through this weekend unscathed. It took several seconds for her eyes to adjust to the dimness of the room. When they finally did, she barely contained her gasp.

Lounging there, his arms spread across the back of an oversized couch, was the largest, most exotic-looking man she had ever seen. His hair was black, and appeared to be cut close to his head. Thick, dark eyebrows were perched over eyes more oval than round, with a slightly flat nose that led down to lips so full and sensual that any woman would want to kiss them. Even her, who'd never been attracted to a man before.

Licking her suddenly dry lips, she forced her gaze away from what was tempting her, and discovered his shoulders took up over half the couch and his chest... his completely naked chest... had muscles on top of muscles.... They couldn't be natural... could they? Her eyes followed those muscles down passed his washboard abs. She discovered his pants were hanging open with a barely covered bulge there that had her eyes widening.

No way! That wasn't humanly possible.

"Come to me, Kristy."

The deep voice had her channel clenching as she ripped her gaze away from the man's cock to find eyes so dark that they didn't seem to have pupils. Was that possible? It had to be a trick of the light, yet there was something in his gaze that made her want to obey him. She found herself unconsciously moving toward him.

∞ ∞ ∞ ∞ ∞

Kirall watched as Dacke's female approached. Dacke had repeatedly told him that she would satisfy his Beast. Looking at her now, Kirall wasn't so sure. She was smaller than Dacke had described, and her hair had none of the white stripes that so enthralled Dacke.

Kirall hated that he would have to rush this first joining. It wasn't his way. He liked females, liked their softness and the sweet smell of their arousal. He liked to taste it, and enjoyed the way it would coat his tongue, knowing the female's desire for him was what had caused it. But he couldn't do that with this female, not with this first joining. His Heat had come on too fast, and he needed to ease it or his Beast would rampage.

"Come, Kristy," he ordered again, watching her intently. The bolus they had given her should have taken effect by now. Not only did the drug make the female more receptive to the differences in the males she was seeing, it also gave the curators a point where they could start altering the memories of her time spent with them.

"Do you need another drink?" she asked, looking from the empty glass on a side table to the bar across the room.

Kirall frowned at the question. He could smell her arousal. She shouldn't be hesitating. Dacke had assured him she was a very receptive female. He needed her to be, if he was going to keep his Beast under control. Perhaps the drug just needed a little more time. He could give her a few more moments.

"Yes," he growled and watched her quickly pick up the glass and move to fill it. The view of her backside had his Beast panting. The clothing they had given her, an extremely short skirt that barely covered the pale globes of her ass, tempted him to pull them apart, impaling her on his shaft knowing her screams of pleasure would soothe his Beast. When she turned, the dim lighting made the sheer top she wore nonexistent, revealing the round tops of generous breasts that made his mouth water as he thought of feeding from them, of nibbling on them, of biting…

"Here you are…" Autumn's words trailed off as she stood in front of him, holding out the glass.

"Kirall," he inserted.

"Kirall… is there anything else…?" Before she could finish her sentence, he knocked the glass out of her hand, and she found herself straddling his lap as he ground his hips against her.

"What are you… stop that!" she demanded, slapping at his chest.

"I will not harm you." Kirall captured both her wrists in one hand, pressing the heel of hers against his chest, as his other hand slipped under her skirt, gripping a bare hip to keep her pinned against him. "Do not struggle, my Beast is close, and he will see it as a challenge."

"Beast..." Autumn immediately froze, her eyes rapidly searching the room. She'd been attacked by a Beast before.

"Yes... I will make sure he does not harm you, but you must obey me." Kirall's Beast had never become so demanding so quickly before. Only in battle would he emerge like this, and only when the need to protect and conquer was dire.

"What must I do?" Autumn whispered softly, keeping all fear from her voice. The Beast would thrive on her fear. He would enjoy her screams of terror and pain.

"Touch me," he ordered.

Slowly, Autumn lowered the hands that she had been trying to keep from touching him, so her palms pressed against his chest as she spread her fingers out as wide as she could with her wrists still restrained. Kirall's response was instantaneous. His muscles rippled, his eyes narrowed, and his nostrils flared.

"Good... That's so good... More," he demanded. "Put your mouth on me."

"I... " She watched as his dark eyes began to turn golden, and his jaw changed shape at her hesitation. "My hands... You have my hands," she quickly whispered, suddenly realizing the Beast he was talking about wasn't in the room but was in him. What the hell had Kristy gotten her into?!!

Kirall's eyes watched her as if she were prey, searching for any reason to pounce as he slowly released her wrists. Moving her hands to his sides, Autumn carefully leaned forward, lowering her mouth to his chest. A rumble seemed to resonate from deep within him. It moved through her body, stirring things up inside her the way thunder did as it rolled across the plains, warning of an approaching storm.

"More," he demanded, his hips moving harder against hers.

Opening her mouth, Autumn slowly swiped her tongue over a bulging muscle, shocked at his sweet, yet spicy taste, finding

20

she wanted more. Moving slowly, she dragged her tongue over the contours of his massive chest, taking her time at each flat, brown nipple, before reaching the pulse that throbbed at the base of his neck. Grazing her teeth over the bulging vein, she found herself lightly nipping at it before closing her lips on it to suck.

∞ ∞ ∞ ∞ ∞

Kirall's Beast roared inside him that this female dared to tease him. For her to pretend to bite him, to feed on him, and then to heal him? Sliding a finger under the thin piece of fabric that separated him from her lair, he felt her wetness and knew she wanted him. Ripping the offending fabric away, he began to stroke her, coating his fingers in the slickness of her arousal before probing her entrance.

Autumn gasped at his intimate touch. Feeling her channel clench and tighten, she cried out as her nails raked along his sides, "No!"

"Yes! Give me your sounds!" he demanded. Capturing her wrists again, he trapped them against her sides, then lifting her, he positioned his cock at her entrance. "Don't tempt the Beast," he growled, pulling her down as he thrust up into her.

Throwing her head back, Autumn couldn't stop the scream that erupted from her throat.

Kirall closed his eyes as the female gasped, and cried out in pleasure as she rode his cock. It soothed his Beast even as he tried to bore deeper into her channel. Kur be praised! He had never felt such a hot, tight cunt before. He had thought better of Dacke. It didn't feel as if he had ever entered this snug nest. When the female's cries finally turned to whimpers, he knew she had found her release, and he erupted into her depths with a roar.

∞ ∞ ∞ ∞ ∞

Autumn's chin dropped to her chest, and she squeezed her eyes shut, trying to stop her tears. She'd just lost her innocence to some big fucking alien. That's the only thing Kirall could be, because human eyes didn't change color.

Her mother had told her that her first time should be with the man she married, the man she loved. Because it was a gift. One she could only give once, and that they would be bound together, forever, if it was with someone you loved. The way her parents had been.

Now she would never have that special bond, and she wanted to scream and rail! After everything else she'd had to survive, how could this have been taken from her too!

And it was all Kirall's fault!

Autumn's sense of fair play chose that moment to kick in.

She was the one that had pretended she was Kristy.

Kirall had never seen Kristy before, so he wouldn't have known they were different women. Or that Autumn had been a virgin.

Kristy was really the guilty one here. She had to know that Dacke would be expecting her to have sex with him. It just served her purpose to not tell her, just like she hadn't told her about the pill they would demand she take. Kristy knew Autumn would never have agreed if she had known. It had been the subject of a very lengthy conversation one night when Autumn had cramps, and refused to take Kristy's prescription medication.

Yes, Kristy had set both of them up. Her and Kirall. Autumn would deal with her... If she survived this weekend.

∞ ∞ ∞ ∞ ∞

Kirall couldn't remember ever having achieved such a release. This female's responses had soothed his Beast in a way he didn't understand, while her tightness had driven him mad. His cock had swollen despite her tightness, and locked him inside her while his seed searched for a place to plant his young. It would not find one, because Dragoons could only impregnate their mate, and there was no way this female could be his mate. He growled deeply when the female began to move without his permission.

"Remain still!" he ordered.

"My fingers are going numb," she whispered.

Opening his eyes, Kirall was surprised to find the female had bowed her head in respect to his Beast. Looking at her hands, he found her fingers were indeed turning white from lack of circulation. Releasing them, he frowned at the bruises forming around her wrists. Looking to her pale hips, he found bruises were forming there too.

"I need to move," Autumn told him, then gasped in pain as she tried to rise.

Kirall's hands quickly encircled her waist, stilling her movements. "It will be several more minutes before the swelling goes down."

"Swelling???" Autumn glanced up at him, then quickly looked away, continuing to try and wiggle free.

"Stop!" His hands tightened enough to hold her still, but not enough to do harm. "You will injure yourself." The sudden scent of blood filling the air had his nostrils flaring. Lowering his head, he inhaled deeply and searched for the source. With stunned eyes, he watched a thin trickle of blood combined with his seed emerge from her lair before it traveled down the length of his cock she hadn't been able to take. His Beast howled at the sweet aroma. Kirall wrapped his arms around her back, continuing to hold her in place as his fingers wrapped around the curls flowing down her back. Pulling on them, he forced her head up.

"Look at me!" he demanded, and was shocked when green eyes streaked with amber met his, instead of the blue ones Dacke had gone on and on about. "You are not Kristy!" he growled, and saw the truth shimmering in her green eyes. "Who are you?!?"

"Au… Autumn," she stuttered.

Kirall's growl grew as she raised her chin ever so slightly, challenging his Beast. He would have risen and moved away from her, protecting her from his Beast, if his cock weren't still lodged deep inside her tight cunt… tight… so tight… his eyes widened as he remembered her cries… her screams. Kur! They hadn't been from pleasure, as he and his Beast had both assumed. They had been from fear… and pain… both caused by him penetrating her boundary. He could see the evidence in the tracks her tears had left on her face. Carefully, gently, he wiped them away with his thumbs.

"This was your first joining," he tried to speak softly, but the words came out as a harsh rumble, his eyes narrowing as he waited for her answer.

"Yes." Autumn knew she couldn't lie to him, not with the evidence dripping out of her. Her response had Kirall hissing, and she watched as his muscular chest seemed to take on a life of its own.

"Touch me!" he ordered, then growled when she didn't move. "Touch me now! Soothe my Beast or he will take over!"

Kirall's dark eyes bored into hers, and she watched in stunned fascination as gold began to fill them, and his features started to shift.

"Touch me, now!" This time, his words were barely recognizable.

Trembling, Autumn placed her hands on his heaving chest, spreading her fingers out as wide as possible. Soothing him. Slowly, the gold began to recede to just the rims of his eyes, and his features settled back into his almost-human form.

Kirall's intense gaze watched the human female as he partially shifted. He could scent her fear, but it wasn't overpowering, and it didn't stop her from doing what was necessary to help him control his Beast. How her mere touch was able to accomplish this, he did not yet understand. But he would, he must, or his Beast would never give him a moment's peace.

"Why are you here?" he demanded, then growled as she started to lift her hands. "Don't! He is barely content."

Autumn watched Kirall carefully as she returned her palms to his chest. His muscles moved under them as if something was trying to rub against her.

"Is he always like this?" The question slipped out before she could stop it.

"No." Kirall frowned, feeling his Beast's contentment at her touch. "It must be the Joining Heat." His eyes flashed at her. "Now tell me why you are here, and not Kristy."

"She... Kristy's couldn't come," Autumn began.

"That doesn't explain why you are here," he told her impatiently.

25

"I'm getting to that!" Autumn's response shocked not only herself, but Kirall as well. "Kristy spent the advance money you gave her, and was worried she would get in trouble if she didn't show up. So she begged me to take her place. We're roommates. We look enough alike that she didn't think anyone would notice."

"How were you able to get through testing without them discovering you had never joined?"

"I...what testing?" Autumn frowned at him. "I arrived, gave them Kristy's I.D. and paperwork, and they took me directly to a room and told me to change into this." Autumn looked down at her uniform, and was shocked to find it destroyed. She hadn't even realized he'd shredded it.

"You went through no scans?" his words drew her eyes back to his. "Were given no bolus?"

"Bolus?" she questioned.

"You put it in your mouth," he told her in a frustrated voice, "and swallow it." He saw guilt fill her eyes. "Aud-um..."

"I didn't take it," she told him angrily. "I react badly to medication."

"You would not have been allowed further if you refused to take it." When she tried to look away, he gripped her chin refusing to allow it. "Aud-um!"

"I stuck it under my tongue, and when that creep, Bonn, wasn't looking I spit it out," she lifted her chin defiantly.

Kirall closed his eyes, growling his displeasure, even as his Beast enjoyed her craftiness.

"Why? Bonn said it was just something to give me more energy." Looking at him, she saw that had been a lie and demanded, "What does it actually do?"

"It... makes the female more accepting of the... differences between the males at the gathering and a human male," Kirall told her carefully.

"Accepting... You mean it makes them want to have sex!" Her accusation hung heavy in the air, irritating his Beast that was just starting to settle.

"It causes them to do nothing they would not normally do!" Kirall denied. "It only enables the female to overlook the male's differences when he chooses her to join with."

"What 'differences'?" Autumn demanded.

"There are many different species of males in the universe, each with varying requirements for joining. At a gathering, a male will sample the females until he finds one that can satisfy his unique needs. Gatherings on Earth are new, as we've only been traveling in this area for the last several hundred years. But they've quickly become highly prized."

"Why?" she looked at him suspiciously.

"Because your females are very... adaptable. You have more orifices than most, and are willing to use them all. Many are not. That means more males are able to join and find relief, even though they are a great distance from their own females."

"Kristy never told me any of that. She only said that a man named Dacke stopped others from bothering her. I wouldn't have come had I known it meant I had to have sex."

"You would never have been invited," Kirall told her bluntly. "Only single, experienced females are allowed at a gathering. The curator should have confirmed your identity.

"Why?" she asked. "Why Kristy?"

"Because she greatly satisfied Dacke. Not only with her willingness to use all her orifices, but also with the appreciative sounds she would make during their joining. Many heard these sounds, and wished to sample her, but Dacke refused."

Autumn found herself blushing as she realized what Kirall meant. Kristy was definitely a screamer during sex. On more than one occasion, she had been woken by Kristy's 'sounds'.

"Only a male that has sampled a female can invite her to return," Kirall's words brought Autumn's attention back to him.

"But she has no memory of her… joining with him."

"That is because they were altered. As yours will be."

"Altered…"

"You will remember nothing of your time here… except that it was… pleasant." Kirall found that he didn't like that. Neither did his Beast who began to move beneath his skin.

"But you will," Autumn whispered. "You will remember everything we did in this room. Just like this Dacke does with Kristy."

"Of course."

"So why was I taken to you and not Dacke? You and Kristy…" Autumn trailed off finding that thought bothered her.

"No, Dacke was to join with her again, but somehow your moon triggered my Joining Heat. When Dacke discovered this, he offered me Kristy, because he knew she would be able to satisfy my needs."

"Your needs…." Autumn felt like a broken record.

"Yes. I am a Prime Dragoon, Dacke is a Minor Dragoon. He understands that my need to join would cause me to capture all the females at the gathering until I found one that could satisfy me." He shrugged at Autumn's shocked look. "It is a trait of the heat to take first and ask later."

"Yeah, I discovered that," Autumn muttered, then stiffened when Kirall was suddenly nose-to-nose with her and growled.

"You were not invited!" he roared, as black scales formed on his elongating face, and his teeth lengthened to deadly sharp points.

Screaming, Autumn shoved against his expanding chest, and found she was suddenly on the floor with a massive half-man, half-Beast towering over her.

# Chapter Three

Dacke remained hidden deep in the shadows, frowning as the door closed behind the last group of females. Kristy hadn't been in any of the groups. How was that possible? He'd only wanted to get a glimpse of her, to see if she was really as beautiful as he remembered. But with her not arriving, he had a bigger problem than finding a female to satisfy *him*. He needed to find one that could satisfy a Prime Dragoon in the midst of his Joining Heat.

He needed to get to Kirall, and let him know Kristy hadn't arrived. Something he wasn't looking forward to, especially since he'd vowed she would be able to satisfy him. Then he would have to find a female who could. He just hoped Kirall would let him live long enough to do that.

∞ ∞ ∞ ∞ ∞

Kirall tried to control his Beast, but the idea of her forgetting them while the combined scent of their blood and seed still hung in the air, along with her challenging words and attempt to escape, made it impossible.

Kirall's Battle Beast stood over nine feet tall, its skin covered with the thick, black, impenetrable scales of his Dragon. Long, sharp claws burst from his fingers, and his clothing fell away as he rose. His roar was so loud that the room shook.

Autumn tried to scoot away from the enraged Beast, but her movements drew its golden gaze. It dropped to its knees, grabbed her ankles, and she screamed.

"You should not have run, little Aud-um," the Beast growled in a deep, gravelly voice that while still Kirall's, seemed to be coming from the bottom of a deep, dark pit. "Now, I will have you!"

Autumn whimpered when the Beast began to slowly pull her toward him, lowering his massive head filled with razor-sharp teeth. Closing her eyes, she waited for the remembered pain of a different beast's bite. Instead, the sweep of a warm, wet tongue along her inner thigh had her gasping, and her eyes flew open.

"So sweet..." the Beast growled softly, as he lapped at the combination of his seed and her barrier.

∞ ∞ ∞ ∞ ∞

Autumn shivered when his rough tongue traveled further up her thigh, consuming every drop before switching to her other leg. She stiffened as his continued growls of pleasure suddenly turned menacing when his tongue reached the scars on that leg. The sound caused more fluid to escape from her, and the Beast's attention was immediately drawn to the fresh juice. He began to lick her like she was his favorite treat.

"Oh..." Having risen to her elbows, Autumn's head fell back when his tongue stiffened and pressed into her. She could feel every inch of that long tongue as it moved in and out, curling around itself, capturing more juice before bringing it back to swallow. His deep rumbles of pleasure vibrated against her clit as he swallowed, sending wave after wave of new sensations through her. Surely she couldn't be getting turned on by this... but when his tongue found a spot deep inside her that she didn't even know existed and rubbed, her womb clenched, and her thighs clamped on his head holding him in place while her hips instinctively started to pump.

Kirall's growls grew at her response. His tongue continued to attack that sweet spot, showing her no mercy. He felt her

31

tighten around him, and she flooded his mouth with more of her sweet juice. He would have her release. He would have her screams of pleasure, never of pain, never again.

Gasping, Autumn's fingers dug into Kirall's scalp, her body curling around his head as her body tightened to the point of pain. Her hips pumped furiously against his mouth, and she didn't care if his teeth shredded her or not. She had to have this. Had to have whatever this was or die! Then, with one final stroke of his tongue, her body imploded.

∞ ∞ ∞ ∞ ∞

Kirall's Beast consumed the last of Autumn's juices as her tremors subsided. He retreated entirely satisfied, and finally relinquished control back to Kirall, allowing dark eyes not golden ones, to meet the dazed green of hers. His eyes hardened when he saw the teeth marks left on her lower lip. They told him she had withheld her sounds from him.

"I am not pleased with you, little Aud-um. You didn't give me your sounds. You will give them to me! I will have everything!"

Before Autumn could respond, there was a pounding on the door.

"Kirall!"

"Go away!" Kirall recognized Dacke's voice, but his eyes remained on Autumn.

"There's a problem. I need to enter."

"No!" Kirall surged to his feet. Gold began rimming his eyes again as he placed a protective leg on either side of Autumn. "I will kill whoever enters!"

∞ ∞ ∞ ∞ ∞

Autumn swallowed hard at the view she was getting. Kirall's cock was nearly as thick as her wrist, and growing as adrenaline pumped through him, his balls hanging heavily below it.

*Damn, if Kirall didn't have a pair*, she thought.

Autumn forced her eyes away, and tried to listen to what was going on outside the door. Hearing the word replace, she watched in astonishment as Kirall seemed to grow even larger than before. Black scales started covering his body, and claws extended from his fingers. Someone would die if he didn't calm, and that someone would most likely be her.

"Kirall..." Speaking in a soft but firm voice, she carefully placed a hand on the massive calf that was closest to her. He had said that she calmed his Beast. Hopefully, she could now.

Kirall's head whipped down at her touch, and found pleading eyes.

"Calm," her eyes pleaded with his nearly golden ones. "He must have finally looked at the paperwork, and realized I'm not Kristy. You have to let him in."

"No!" he growled, but the gold started receding from his eyes as he regained control of his Beast. "They will not see you like this." His eyes traveled over her nearly-naked body. He didn't know why the thought of another male seeing her like this bothered him, but it did.

"Kirall!" Dacke shouted again.

"Give me a dracking moment!" he shouted, but in a more normal voice as he extended a now claw-free hand to Autumn.

Slowly, Autumn took it, watching him closely as he helped her to her feet.

"Go into the cleansing area." He pointed to a door on the other side of the room. "Close the door, and remain there until I tell you to come out."

Autumn quickly nodded, then slowly backed away from him until she bumped into the door. Reaching behind her, she found the handle then slid inside, slamming the door shut.

Kirall watched Autumn until she was safely inside the cleansing room. He knew why Dacke was here, to replace her. His Beast rumbled his displeasure, and Kirall found for once he was in total agreement with his Beast. He wasn't done with this little female, not even close.

∞ ∞ ∞ ∞ ∞

Dacke jumped back, ready to defend himself when the door to Kirall's lair was suddenly yanked open. He had expected to find an enraged Battle Beast ready to rampage because Kristy hadn't been brought to him.

Instead, he found a very naked and very angry Kirall.

"My Lord." He quickly bowed his head to the Prime.

"What is so urgent that you dare to interrupt me, Dacke?" Kirall demanded.

"My Lord … there is a problem. Kristy did not arrive." Dacke glanced up and away, quickly continuing when Kirall's eyes narrowed. "I will find you a willing female. It will just take a little time."

"I don't need one," Kirall told him.

"I… but…" Shock had Dacke looking Kirall in the eye. "Your Heat has subsided?"

"No. Bonn brought me a female, one he thought was your Kristy, but she is nothing like you described. She is more, much, much more."

"I don't understand," Dacke frowned. "How is it possible for Bonn not to have known?"

"It seems he failed to verify her identity. He also did not test her."

"What?!! How do you know this?"

"She told me, after I realized she couldn't be Kristy."

"How did you..." Dacke trailed off as he suddenly smelled blood, boundary blood. They had always been told that they would recognize its unique scent if they were ever so honored to receive it. It was a sweet scent that still hung heavy in the air.

That was how Kirall had known the female wasn't Kristy. He had breached an innocent's boundary. They had also been taught that it should never be done during a Joining Heat because a male tended to lose control.

"The female..." he hesitated to ask but his honor demanded it. "Do I need to summon the Healer?"

Kirall's Beast rippled beneath his skin, angered that a Minor would question him so, but Kirall understood his friend's concern, and admired that his honor demanded he worry about a female he did not know.

"No, she is fine." Kirall frowned, remembering the bruises he'd left on her skin. He would have to be more careful with her. "What you need to do is discover the extent of Bonn's incompetence. If he can't be trusted to enforce the simple guidelines he was given, that only experienced females are allowed at a gathering, then he will need to be replaced."

"Agreed," Dacke growled, wondering if this had happened to any other females. He began to turn away then paused needing to be sure. "She satisfies you? This innocent?"

He'd never heard of such a thing, only experienced females were able to satisfy a male during a Heat.

"More than you can imagine," Kirall told him moving to shut the door. "Now leave, I have been away from her for too long, and feel my Heat rising."

∞ ∞ ∞ ∞ ∞

Dacke stared at the door to Kirall's temporary lair, still stunned at what he had learned. An innocent female was able to satisfy a Prime during his Heat. He never would have believed it if anyone other than Kirall had told him. He'd seen how quickly the Heat had come on, and how desperate Kirall had been. Still, she never should have been granted entrance.

He needed to find out how it had happened, who was responsible, and make sure it never happened again. But first he needed to make sure every other female had been tested.

Spinning on his heel, he stormed down the corridor, never seeing the figure hiding in the shadows.

∞ ∞ ∞ ∞ ∞

Keeping an eye on the closed door, Autumn took in the room she'd been sent to. It seemed to be your typical bathroom only on a larger scale. Looking across the room, she froze. There, standing on the other side of the room, was a creature she barely recognized. Moving slowly, she approached the mirror and took in her ravished appearance. Her tears had destroyed the makeup Kristy had applied, and the hair so carefully styled to look wild, now truly was.

While she hadn't liked the outfit they'd given her to wear, at least it had partially covered her. Now the skirt was gone and the see-through top was shredded, even her bra only had one strap left. Ripping both off, she let them fall to the floor and examined her body. Her chest was slightly red from rubbing against Kirall's, but it wasn't too bad. Turning sideways, she could see the bruises forming on her hips and wrists from his strong grip. All in all, it could have been a hell of a lot worse.

Looking deep into the green eyes reflected back at her, she forced herself to face what had happened, because nothing could change it. She couldn't regain her innocence, couldn't go back to not knowing that there really were aliens out there.

If one good thing had come from this, at least she knew she wasn't crazy. If there were men like Kirall that could change into large Beasts, maybe there were those that turned into lizards too. It was a question she needed answered before Kirall sent her away, because obviously he would.

His words had said it all. He wasn't pleased with her. Autumn felt her anger start to burn. Not pleased... that big, fucking alien had taken her virginity, given her her first orgasm, then dared to claim that she hadn't pleased him! Where did he get off?!! And he had! Even when she hadn't, he had, and she knew it because he had licked it out of her.

'Not pleased my ass!' she thought. If anyone had the right to bitch it was her!

Then he thought he had the right to demand that she give him everything? What had he given her? Nothing! She wouldn't even remember any of this if what he said was true. Autumn looked to the still closed door.

Fuck him! Let him replace her. She didn't care. She'd survived worse things than this in her life, but she'd be damned if she was going to go looking like this!

Turning, she stomped into the oversized shower and turned on all the jets.

∞ ∞ ∞ ∞ ∞

Entering the cleansing room, Kirall frowned. She wasn't there. The remnants of her clothes were, but there was no sign of Autumn. His frown deepened when he realized the water was running. He hadn't told her she could cleanse. This little female needed to learn to obey him, and he knew just how to teach her. Smiling, he moved to the cleansing unit.

What he found when he entered the stall nearly stole his breath. Autumn was facing him, her head tilted back, her eyes closed as she massaged foam into her hair. Tendrils of the foam traveled down her lush body, hugging every curve before disappearing between her sweet thighs, reappearing as they curled their way around her legs before reluctantly ending their journey by caressing her petite feet.

How could one tiny Earth female have captivated him so? He was in his Joining Heat, and should have accepted the offer to have her replaced. She was inexperienced and innocent in the ways to truly satisfy a male. Yet, she had satisfied not only him, but his Beast as well. She'd even caused his Dragon to lift its head with interest. That was something that never should have happened unless he was with his mate. He needed to find out why. He needed her to give him her sounds so he could understand.

"I am not pleased with you, little Aud-um," he growled softly, and watched her hands still before she slowly finished removing the foam from her hair that now glowed like the darkest of fires. His Dragon sat up wanting to see more. Slowly, she opened her eyes, and stared directly into his without one ounce of fear or submission.

"First of all," she raised a finger, "if you're going to come into someone's shower uninvited, you should at least know her name. It's Autumn! Not Aud-um." She raised a second finger. "Second, I get that you're not pleased with me, but guess what?

38

I'm not pleased with you either. No one asked me if I wanted to be the sex toy for some frigging alien in heat. Third." There were now three fingers in Kirall's stunned face as she took a step toward him. "My 'sounds' are mine. To be given to whom I choose, when I choose. They can never be demanded! When I find a male that's worthy of them, then he'll get them, every... single... one. And guess what, Kirall... when that happens, we will both remember it. You've taken enough. Now get out of my way so I can dry off. I'm sure you're anxious to get to a female that *will* please you!" Shoving him aside, she stormed out of the stall.

Kirall couldn't move. He was stunned. No one stood up to a Prime Dragoon like that, not even a Prime female. Yet this little Earth female wasn't intimidated by him or by his Beast. She even dared to challenge them, claiming they weren't worthy to hear her sounds of pleasure. She dared to suggest, to his face, that another male would be. All three parts of him growled in anger. He would show her just what happened when you challenged a Prime Dragoon!

Turning, he stormed out of the stall only to have his breath stolen yet again. She stood with her back to him, a towel wrapped around her hair, lifting it, while another wrapped around her body, concealing her curves. But it was what the towels didn't conceal that stunned him. Scars. Rows and rows of scars crisscrossed her shoulder blades before disappearing under the towel. Growling, he took two steps toward her and ripped the towel from her body, revealing that the scars traveled all the way down to her hips, as if some crazed Beast had savaged her.

"What the fuck do you think you're doing?" she demanded.

"You've been damaged!" His gaze flew to hers in the mirror, capturing it. He saw the shock and pain that filled her eyes before it was replaced by anger.

Shit, she'd forgotten about the scars. Whipping around, she grabbed for the towel. "Give me that!" she demanded not realizing that the mirror continued to reveal her back.

"Who damaged you?!!" he demanded. "Why were you never properly treated?" All three parts of him were equally enraged! She was one that never should have been harmed. She was one who should have been protected at all costs.

Autumn stiffened at his words. She knew just how damaged she was, and not all of the scars were external. She'd been this way since she was ten, but that didn't mean she needed some big, overgrown alien telling her she was.

"That's none of your damn business!" she exclaimed.

"You will tell me!" Kirall demanded.

"No," she said between gritted teeth. "I... will... not! And just so you know, they were properly repaired."

"If they were, you wouldn't still have them!" Kirall all but roared, getting nose-to-nose with her.

"Well, sorry to displease you, yet again," she snapped back. "Now give me that towel! I want out of here!"

"You will go nowhere!" he roared.

"Oh yes, I will." When he still refused to release her towel, she grabbed the one from her hair and wrapped it around her body. "I'm sure my replacement is damage free, and more than willing to scream on demand. I, on the other hand, am going to go find me a male who will not only give me his sounds, but will give me all of him, and that's something you will never do, will you, Kirall?" With that, she stormed out of the room.

Kirall just stood there for a moment, stunned by her challenge. No female could accept all three parts of a Prime

Dragoon, especially one as tiny as her. Only his mate would be able to do this, for his Dragon would rip apart any other female.

Yet just the thought of her wanting to try had his Heat rising, along with his anger. He may not be able to give her all of him, but by Kur, he'd make sure he gave her something no other male could!

∞ ∞ ∞ ∞ ∞

Autumn released an angry shriek when she found herself suddenly flying through the air before landing on a huge, soft bed.

"What the fuck!" she demanded.

"Oh, we will, little Aud-um, that I promise you," Kirall growled, his large body instantly on top of her, pressing her face down into the bed as he growled in her ear. "I told you before not to run."

"I wasn't *running*," she stressed the word as she struggled beneath, discovering that while he wasn't letting her up, he wasn't crushing her either. "I was *leaving*. There's a difference."

"Not to my Beast."

"That's your Beast's problem, not mine. Now get off me." Pressing her hands into the bed, she shoved up with all her might, ignoring the wave of disappointment that filled her when Kirall allowed it, willing to let her go.

*Of course he would*, she thought, *she was damaged*. She quickly discovered he only let her up far enough to rip away her towel.

"Now, little Aud-um, we fuck!" he told her as he rose to his knees, lifting her hips so her legs were on either side of his hips and his cock could slide up between the beautiful globes of her ass. When the mounds immediately tightened around his cock, he groaned.

41

"No way in hell!" Autumn exclaimed, pushing up off the bed, trying to jerk away.

"But I thought you wanted all of me, little Aud-um," he growled, pulling on her hips so she fell back onto her elbows.

"Not up my ass! Are you crazy?!! You're huge!" she shouted, still struggling only to find she couldn't move unless she wanted to face-plant in the bed again.

"Then maybe you should be more careful what you ask for. You just might get it," he whispered darkly before pulling back so his cock slid downward between the silky folds concealing the entrance of her nest. Already he could smell her arousal, could feel her slickness coating his cock. His little Aud-um did want to fuck, which was good because so did he.

Positioning his cock at her entrance, he thrust into her then instantly froze hearing her gasp. Kur! This heat and his anger were making him forget that she was an innocent, that she would be sore from their first joining.

"Aud-um?" he asked gruffly, his body trembling as he resisted the overpowering urge of his Heat that demanded he think only of himself, and plunge ruthlessly into her swollen folds. He had done that during their first joining, and had hurt her. He refused to do that again. He was a Prime Dragoon. He would not be ruled by his Heat.

"Just... just give me a minute," she gasped out, panting.

Slowly he felt her start to relax beneath him, and knew he had proven that he was stronger than his Heat. At least until she moved, taking him even deeper, then the Heat blasted through him annihilating his control.

"Kur!" he cursed. Tightening his grip on her hips, he began thrusting rapidly into her nest, finding it was even hotter and tighter than before.

"Oh!" Autumn cried out, her fingers digging into the sheets as she pressed her face deeper into the bed. The pleasure of what he was doing overwhelming her.

"Yes!" Kirall called out driving even deeper into her. "Give me your sounds!" Already he could feel his balls tightening, pulling up close against his body as his release drew near, but he needed more. He needed her to find pleasure too. Reaching around her, he found her clit and began working it furiously. Her muffled sounds telling him she liked what he was doing, but it was her channel that told him the most. It was nearly strangling his cock with its tight hot grip as it tried to keep him inside her.

Kur! It was the most incredible thing he'd ever felt. Never had a nest felt so good. So right.

"Kirall!" she cried out into the bed.

With her channel convulsing around him, Kirall could hold back no longer. With one final thrust that embedded him deep inside her, he reared back holding her so tightly against the base of his cock, that it was as if they were one being. With a roar, his seed flooded her womb.

∞ ∞ ∞ ∞ ∞

Rattler entered the 'selection room', as he and Bonn had come to call it. It was where all the women invited to the gatherings were brought after being tested and drugged. They would walk from table to table, thinking they were taking drink orders when in reality the aliens were assessing them, and choosing which one they would fuck first.

It wasn't uncommon for a woman to end up with five or six different aliens over the course of the weekend. This Kristy was the only one he knew of that hadn't been shared among the aliens. She was also the only one he'd ever heard of being asked to return.

If what he'd overheard was true, she'd had someone take her place. Someone who had been a virgin, and the aliens knew about it. He needed to find Bonn and tell him. Seeing him at the bar, he quickly made his way over.

"We have a problem," he told Bonn.

# Chapter Four

Autumn lay on her side breathing hard, a leg thrown over one of Kirall's, while his arm and cock kept them locked together. Before he'd collapsed, he'd rolled them to their sides, and for that Autumn was grateful.

Her mind wasn't fully functioning yet, wasn't processing everything she had just experienced. She'd fully expected to find another woman waiting for Kirall when she'd stormed out of the cleansing room. Instead, she'd been launched across the room and all but ravished by an angry alien.

It was her own fault. She knew that. Who challenged a guy more than three times her size? One that could change into something even bigger. It wasn't the smartest thing she'd ever done. She should have just kept her mouth shut and taken it, like she always did, but for some reason she couldn't.

She was tired of just surviving. Was tired of always having to back down. Of having to just accept everything that had happened to her. She was ready to fight back, even if it hurt, and experience everything life had to offer.

Her parents had always told her she was a fighter, that she had a great inner strength. She lost it that night so many years ago. It seemed to just curl up somewhere deep inside her and disappear. Now... here... it seemed to be returning, and Autumn was going to do whatever it took to keep it.

She had to be honest with herself and admit that when she'd gotten over the shock of it all, she'd enjoyed what Kirall had done to her. If this was what sex was normally like, then she understood why Kristy screamed. The feel of Kirall's cock moving inside her, of him pounding into her as his fingers played with her clit... it had been amazing. No, more than amazing... it had been life changing. She would never be the same girl that had arrived just hours ago.

She had tried to play with her clit before, had tried to masturbate the way all the books said you could, but she'd never been able to. All she'd been able to accomplish was to make herself feel achy and frustrated.

That wasn't the case with Kirall.

Oh, she was achy alright, but in a totally pleasurable way. Shifting slightly, she felt all those sensitive nerve endings spark back to life.

"Cease," Kirall ordered, the arm around her waist tightening, stilling her movements. "I am still too swollen."

"Is it always like this?" she asked quietly.

"No, it is a condition of the Heat. In a normal joining, I would not swell at all."

"So why do you when you are in Heat?"

"It is nature's way of giving my seed the best chance to take root."

"Take root..." she twisted her upper body around giving him a horrified look. "You mean you could get me pregnant?!!" Autumn tried to pull off his cock, but he easily held her in place.

Kirall's eyes narrowed at her expression. He found he did not like the thought that she would be repelled at conceiving his young. "It is a great honor to carry the young of a Prime Dragoon," he told her. "Especially a Black."

"Honor," she snorted. "Right."

Kirall's eyes narrowed even further. "The honor of carrying my young will only be given to my mate," he bit out. "Once I find her, she will be the only female that I will ever join with."

"Oh," Autumn stopped struggling. "So if you can't get me pregnant, why do you swell?"

"As I said, it is a condition of the Joining Heat. It gives a male just the slightest glimpse of the pleasure he will be able to experience with his mate. It is nature's way of hastening his quest to find her."

"I see." She relaxed in his arms. "Do you go into heat a lot?"

"No. A Dragoon only goes into his Joining Heat every hundred years or so."

"Every hundred..." Autumn's eyes widened.

"Yes," he nodded. "This is my fifth heat."

"You're five hundred years old?" She didn't even try to hide her shock.

"No!" he instantly denied. "I am four hundred and forty-six years old."

"But you just said..."

"I know what I said! Somehow your moon triggered my heat. I don't know how, and I don't know why."

"Oh, well, you're still pretty old."

"Not for a Dragoon," he told her.

"Really.... How long can you live?"

"A Dragoon has an unlimited life span. Its length is decided by his mate."

"By his mate?" Autumn gave him a confused look. "I don't understand."

"Do you need to?" Kirall asked impatiently, not liking all these questions. "They are unnecessary and irrelevant because...

"I won't be allowed to remember anything anyway. Right?" she finished for him.

Kirall realized he had spoken aloud, and didn't like the flash of pain he saw in her eyes before she twisted away.

"No, you won't," he softly agreed.

"I'm just here to fuck, right? To relieve your heat." This time when she tried to move, his cock easily slid out of her, and she immediately put some space between them. "So there's really no reason for you to talk to me. When will it hit you again?"

"I do not know," Kirall watched her carefully as he spoke.

"Then I'm going to take a nap. I'm sure you'll wake me when you need to."

∞ ∞ ∞ ∞ ∞

Kirall didn't like how it felt for Aud-um to turn her back on him, even though in reality it had been that way the whole time. This was different though. This was her withdrawing into herself, pulling away from him without moving an inch, and somehow putting a wall up between them.

He silently watched as the stiffness gradually left her body as she relaxed into sleep. He'd hurt her again, this time with his words, and that hadn't been his intention.

He let his gaze travel over the scars that riddled her back. Releasing the claws from his fingers and thumb, he carefully placed them just above her scars and frowned. These scars had been created by a species with only three claws.

If she were Dragoon, his first thought would have been that a Varana had attacked her. But she wasn't Dragoon. So she posed no threat to them. They would have no reason to harm her. Also, her fragile body would never have survived such an attack. Varanian claws would have ripped her apart as they did Dragoon young who were yet unable to shift into their Dragon form.

No, the Varanians couldn't have caused this, but if not them, then what had? And could it happen to her again? He felt his

48

Beast brushing against his skin, rumbling his displeasure at the thought. It wanted to protect Aud-um.

Worried he would disturb the rest she so obviously needed, he slowly rose and began to pace.

Why was his Beast acting this way? It had never happened before. Especially not when Kirall was in a Joining Heat. During his heat, his Beast usually stayed in the background, knowing his appearance could harm the female. And his Dragon... well his Dragon wouldn't be interested in any female that wasn't his mate. If his Dragon were to emerge while Kirall was joining with any other female, he would destroy her.

But with this Heat, his Battle Beast had already made his appearance. He had been enraged when Aud-um had tried to run, and then again when Dacke had interrupted them. The Beast should have rampaged. Should have been uncontrollable. Yet with just a gentle touch and a soft word, Aud-um had been able to calm him.

How had such a little female been able to accomplish this when even a full-grown female Dragoon would have fled when confronted by an enraged Battle Beast.

Not his Aud-um.

And his Dragon?

Why would he be interested in a female so obviously not his mate?

Kirall needed to find out, and if talking to her, and telling her about him and his world achieved that, then he would do it. She wouldn't remember any of it anyway.

Would she?

Kirall came to an abrupt halt, suddenly remembering what she had said. She hadn't taken the bolus. Would the Healer still be able to erase her memories? Without harming her? He didn't know why he never considered it before, that the memory altering might be harmful to a female.

Bonn would have made them aware of it if the females were harmed... wouldn't he? After all, they were human females. Yet the male hadn't even checked Aud-um's paperwork.

Moving to sit in the chair, he continued to think as he watched Aud-um sleep. His chin propped up in his hands, his elbows rested on his knees.

What would happen to his little Aud-um if her memories couldn't be altered?

*His* little Aud-um? She wasn't his!

The sound of a terrified cry, stifled behind tightly sealed lips, had his gaze flying to her sleeping form. Seeing her twitch and jerk, he knew she was having a nightmare. But of what?

Of what had scarred her?

Or was it because of her time spent with him?

∞ ∞ ∞ ∞ ∞

Autumn was instantly awake, but she forced her body to remain absolutely still while her eyes scanned the room, searching for any threat. Finding only Kirall sitting there, watching her, she relaxed slightly. She hadn't meant to fall asleep. She hated sleeping. Sleep brought dreams that were always dark and terrifying, filled with remembered pain and loss. For so many years, she'd been helplessly trapped in those dreams that she would never willingly return.

"What?!!" she asked defensively, pushing back the hair that had fallen over her face.

"You had a nightmare," he told her.

"If you say so."

"Tell me what it was about," Kirall demanded.

"No."

"You will not tell me?" Kirall couldn't believe it.

"No, I'm not here for conversation. Remember? Just to fuck."

"You know, you are very irritating," Kirall leaned back in the chair, his legs spread, seemingly unconcerned with his nakedness or the view he was giving her.

Autumn had never actually gotten a good look at Kirall. Okay, yes, she'd seen his balls and cock up close and personal, but she hadn't really seen all of him, not all at once and not like this.

Damn, the guy was really built.

Trying to corral her wayward thoughts, Autumn shrugged and sat up, trying to act as unconcerned with her nakedness as Kirall seemed to be with his. Just as she opened her mouth to speak, her stomach growled hungrily, and Kirall surged to his feet.

"What was that?!!" he demanded.

"What? The growl?" she asked.

"Yes! Do you have a Beast inside you?"

"No, it was just my stomach." She saw he didn't understand. "I'm hungry. I don't suppose there's anything to eat around here, is there? It's been a long time since breakfast." In fact, Autumn hadn't even gotten that. Not with how long it had taken Kristy to do her hair and makeup. The limo had picked her up at eleven, and after nearly an hour, she'd finally arrived and been brought to Kirall.

"What time is it anyway? How long was I asleep?" She looked to the cheap watch she always wore on her wrist, then remembered she'd left it at the apartment.

"Maybe an hour." Kirall's Beast slowly calmed down as Kirall moved toward the other side of the room. "It is late afternoon."

"Oh."

"There is food."

Kirall gestured to the table Autumn hadn't noticed before. But in her defense, when had she had time to look. Rising from the bed, she leaned down grabbing the towel Kirall had torn from her body. There was no way she was eating naked. Moving into the outer room and to the table he'd gestured to, she saw it was filled with a variety of foods. Some she recognized. Some she didn't.

"Eat whatever you wish," he told her.

Autumn didn't have to be told twice, and began filling a plate with items she recognized. There were meats and cheeses, a mixture of olives and fruits, and there were even cooked shrimp on short wooden skewers. It was like the appetizer table at some fancy party, and for him, she supposed that's exactly what this was. Turning, she found him watching her closely, and her cheeks flushed slightly at how full her plate was. She didn't get to eat like this often, well never really. She mostly existed on peanut butter sandwiches and instant ramen. Occasionally, Fred at the diner would let her have a botched order, but those times were rare because Fred was a tight ass.

"What?" she demanded defensively.

"When did you last eat?" he asked softly.

"I told you..." Autumn turned and looked around the room. It was actually divided into two rooms. One sparsely furnished with a couch, the drink table, and the food table, and one with a bed. A partial wall separated the two.

"Truthfully?" Kirall asked again. "Tell me when."

"Last night after work," she finally told him realizing it was either eat on the bed or on the couch. Choosing the couch, she moved toward it.

"That is not sufficient, not even for one as small as you," Kirall told her.

"Yeah, well not everyone can afford to eat like that." She gestured to the table.

"Food is scarce on your planet?" Kirall frowned, he hadn't been aware of that.

"No, not scarce, but it costs money, and that's something I don't have much of."

"Is that why you willingly took Kristy's place?"

"Partly," she told him absently as she braced the plate on her knees, then popped a big juicy grape into her mouth. "Aren't you going to eat?"

Autumn watched him frown at her, then with one hand he pulled the food-laden table over to the couch, cleared a spot for her plate then took it from her and placed it there. Autumn fought back a smile. Sitting on the couch as she was, the table came up to her chin. It was like being a child again, and trying to sneak a peak at what was on the 'big people's' table.

She let out a startled shriek when Kirall lifted her, settling her across his lap. It brought her up to a normal eating height.

"What is the other part?" he asked. Reaching out he selected a piece of food, then tossed it into his mouth.

Autumn was silent for a moment, trying to decide what she wanted to tell him then shrugged. Did it really matter? It's not like he actually cared. "I want to take night classes."

"Night classes?" he asked.

"Yeah. I finally got my G.E.D., but if I want a better job then I need to learn more."

"G.E.D.?"

"It's kind of like a diploma, but not; for people who didn't go to regular school. You have to have it to get menial jobs. If you want better paying jobs, then you need to take more classes."

"And with a better job, you would be able to eat more often?" Reaching out, he picked out something else and popped it in his mouth before Autumn could warn him.

"Yes. Umm...Kirall," she began, not sure what to do.

"Yes?" he asked, grunting as he chewed.

"You just put a habanero in your mouth."

"So?" he asked, reaching for more.

"They are really hot," she warned.

"They are not bad." He chewed three more. "But they are better than your Fire Water."

"Fire Water?" she asked, confused.

"The drink you gave me. Dacke told me it was called 'Fire Water,' although I do not understand why. It doesn't burn at all."

"Oh, you mean the whiskey. Well, just so you know, you are not kissing me on the mouth after eating all of those."

Kirall's entire being seemed to still, then his gaze trapped hers, and she felt like a bug stuck on a pin.

"I will not be kissing your mouth."

"That... that's what I said," she stuttered, suddenly uncomfortable.

"I will *never* kiss you on your mouth, Aud-um. It is a sacred act, and one I will only ever share with my mate."

"Kissing on the mouth is... sacred for you?" she asked uncertainly.

"Is it not for you?" Kirall was surprised.

"Uh... no... not really," she stuttered. "Why is it so sacred?"

"It is part of the bonding ritual between mates. The sharing of one's life breath with one's mate is... " Kirall inhaled deeply. "It is said to be an amazing experience."

Autumn's eyes widened at the reverence and awe she heard in Kirall's tone. "Is there more to the ritual?"

"Do you really wish to know?" Kirall asked.

"I really do. If you are willing to share it with me."

"If I do, will you tell me how you got your scars?" he asked, because for some reason he really wanted to know. When she jerked trying to rise, he tightened his arms around her, stopping her.

"Let go!" she demanded.

"No." He made her face him. "Why will you not tell me?"

"Because you'll *remember* it!" she spat at him.

"I do not understand," he told her. "Of course, I will."

"But I won't, will I?" she demanded. "You can tell me anything you want. The truth. A lie. And after tomorrow, I won't remember any of it."

"Why does that bother you so?" he asked confused.

"Because I don't want my life… my failures… paraded across the universe long after I'm dead."

"That would never happen!" he immediately denied.

"Right, like no one has heard about how Kristy likes to use all her orifices. Or about how she likes to scream?"

Kirall opened his mouth, then found he had to shut it, for she was right. Stories about Dacke's encounter with Kristy were already spreading far beyond their ship.

"Would you like people talking about you, judging you, long after you were dead?" she demanded.

"No," Kirall admitted quietly. "I would not."

"Then you should understand why I won't tell you."

"I do," he agreed, "but I would still like to know."

"Why?" It was Autumn's turn to question. "Why is it so important to you?"

"I… because it would bring us closer."

"You mean until I leave?" She tilted her head slightly to the side, and gave him a considering look. "You know, I think I envy you."

"What?" Kirall's eyes widened in shock. "Why?"

"Because you can be whoever you want to be right now, and I would never know the difference. You tell me you're a Prime Dragoon," she shrugged her shoulders dismissively, "and who am I to argue? You could tell me your deepest, darkest secrets, and know that they will never be repeated, never be revealed, let alone remembered."

"You think I would lie to you?" Kirall's displeasure at the thought was easily heard.

"I don't know," she told him honestly. "Does it really matter to you what I think? After all, I'm basically just a vessel here to serve your needs."

"That is not how I see you, Autumn," he denied hotly.

"Of course it is, otherwise you'd be willing to talk to me. To tell me about you and your world."

"You are very irritating for an Other. Do you know that?" Kirall asked, reaching out popping another pepper into his mouth.

Autumn just watched Kirall chew. Was he starting to share with her or was it just a slip of the tongue? There was only one way to find out.

"What is an Other?" she asked quietly.

"It is what we call beings like you on my planet."

"Beings like me?" Her eyebrows drew together. "You mean you have humans on your planet?"

"We have beings that are similar to you, although they are larger and much more respectful. They tend the land on our planet, and serve the Dragoons."

"Why?" she asked.

"Why what?" he replied frowning.

"Why do they serve you?"

"Because in return for their work and service, we take them under our protection, and no species dares injure someone under a Dragoon's protection."

"Why do you call them Other?"

"Because that is what they are. Other. They are not like us. They cannot change form and have no Dragon. Therefore, they are Other." He made it sound so simple.

"But I thought you called your Beast a Battle Beast, not a Dragon," Autumn frowned at him.

"I have another form. A Dragon form."

"Seriously? You can honestly turn into a fire-breathing Dragon? With wings and everything?" Excitement filled her voice.

"Of course!" Kirall told her giving her an insulted look.

"Can I see him?" she asked.

"No!" he told her, and immediately the excitement and sparkle in her eyes disappeared.

"Oh, so 'Others' aren't allowed to see you in that form." She didn't try to hide her disappointment.

"Others see us in our Dragon form all the time," Kirall admitted.

"So it's just me." She again tried to pull away from him.

"Yes, but not for the reason you think." He could see the hurt in her eyes as he held her in his lap. "You asked me to be honest with you. Do you only wish that if it pleases you?"

Autumn stopped struggling in his arms. "No. I want you to tell me the truth. I want to for once be… "

"Be?" he asked when she cut herself off.

"Be treated as if I haven't been 'damaged'. To be treated as if I didn't need to be handled 'carefully'. I think I have more than proven that I can handle what life throws at me and survive. Even when it's a horny alien." She gave him a half-hearted smile.

Kirall was silent for a moment, not returning her smile. "I do not know what you have survived, but I do know that you did. And for that I thank Kur."

"Yeah, right." Autumn rolled her eyes. "You wanted Kristy and got me instead." She would have turned away, but Kirall's hand cupping her jaw stopped her, and she found her gaze trapped by two very serious eyes.

"I am very pleased that it was you who arrived instead of Kristy, Autumn."

Her eyes widened because he was suddenly pronouncing her name correctly.

"You have satisfied me, Autumn, in ways I never could have anticipated," he admitted.

"Then why won't you show me your Dragon?" she asked, letting him hear the need that even she didn't understand.

"Because he would destroy you," he told her quietly.

"What?" Her eyes widened in shock.

Kirall sighed heavily. "My Dragon is my preferred form on my home planet. He is very different than my Battle Beast. His wingspan is massive, and he loves to soar high in the sky, protecting his territory and everyone in it. But if he were to emerge while I was joining with a female that was not our mate... he would rip her apart."

"But your Battle Beast didn't hurt me."

"No, he did not, which is surprising. But you were not afraid of him as so many are, so maybe that is the difference."

"Difference?"

"Yes. My Battle Beast has never appeared during any of my other Heats. He is too primal for most females, and they do not welcome his attentions, fearing he will harm them."

"He would never harm me," she denied, feeling the need to defend his Beast.

"You are bruised," Kirall countered, carefully picking up one of her wrists, seeing the bruise that was still there.

"I hate to tell you this, Kirall, but your Beast didn't do that... you did."

Kirall growled his displeasure at her statement. "I know this, Autumn, but what I don't understand is why he didn't, and only you can explain that to me."

"Me? How would I know? As you said, I am an Other, and apparently on your planet they are not useful for anything other than service."

"That is not true, a Dragoon can mate with an Other, but it is not... encouraged."

"What do you mean?"

Kirall settled back into the couch, pulling her with him. "I told you how the length of a Dragoon's life was dependent on its mate."

"Yes, but I don't understand why."

"It is because of the mating bond. It binds them together in a way I cannot explain, but it is for life, and the life of an Other mate is always precarious."

"Why is it so precarious?"

"Because even when strengthened by a Dragoon's kiss and a Dragon's blood, an Other is still fragile and easy to end."

"Kiss and blood?"

"Yes. During the mating process, a Dragoon will bind its life force to its mate's by kissing them on the mouth, sharing their life's breath. Then the Dragoon partially shifts so that his Dragon can join with its mate."

"How can a Dragon possibly join with an Other?" Autumn whispered, discovering that just the thought of joining with Kirall's Dragon had her experiencing her own heat.

"The Dragon bites the Other." His finger gently caressed the juncture at the base of her neck. "Here, taking the Other's blood, allowing it to mix with his before injecting it back into the Other. It binds them together for all eternity."

"But how does a Dragon actually… " Autumn felt her cheeks flush.

"Join with his mate?" he finished for her.

"Yes."

"If the mate is Other, then it can only be accomplished by the Dragon using either his tail or tongue."

"Seriously? I would have thought…"

"Thought what, little Aud-um."

"Well… that a Dragon would have a cock, if he were male, and that he would join with his mate that way."

"He would if she were a Dragoon mate, but he cannot do that with an Other mate. It would kill her."

"Oh."

"There is another deterrent to taking an Other for a mate, for while the Other mate becomes stronger than before, he or she will still not be able to shift. Thus making them unable to protect themselves as well as a Dragoon mate could. It makes both of them more vulnerable to attack. If the Other mate were to die, then the Dragoon mate would retreat into its lair and slowly, painfully fade away."

"What happens if you mate with a Dragoon?"

"While a female Dragoon is harder to kill than an Other, she is still not as strong as a male, and has no Battle Beast.

Therefore, she must be protected. If she were to die, the result for her mate is the same. It is why mates are protected so fiercely, especially the female ones. It is why many Dragoon's refuse to take an Other as their mate."

"I don't understand. If they are mates, how can you refuse to 'mate' with them?"

"As long as the bonding process has not been completed, the Dragoon has a chance to find another mate that is not so... fragile."

"But..."

"Many choose to go through life alone, rather than take on the burden of an Other mate."

"Burden?" Autumn didn't try to hide her shock.

"An Other mate must be guarded fiercely, Autumn. Male or female. For while they are a treasure to their mate, they are also a weakness, and Dragoons do not like weakness. Many will attack the mate, knowing it will kill the Dragoon. It is how we lost the Supremes."

"The Supremes?"

"Prime Dragoons were not always the most powerful of the Dragoons. There were once ones even stronger, ones called Supremes. Many of them found their mates within the Others. It caused many to become jealous, both Dragoon and Other. They plotted against the mates, striking when they were the most vulnerable, until only one Supreme remained, Razeth. He left Mondu in search of his mate and never returned.

"He just disappeared?"

"Yes. No evidence of where he went has ever been found, and with him went our greatest strength."

"What do you mean?"

"There is a hierarchy for Dragoons. I am a Prime. Dacke is a Minor. The higher mate sets your status in our society. If a

Minor mates with another Minor, they cannot become more powerful, but may increase their status. If a Prime mates with a Minor, then the Minor becomes a Prime, more powerful. And there was a time when you could become a Supreme."

"But now you are the most powerful."

"Yes, but our world is a weaker place without the Supremes."

"So are all Primes black like your Battle Beast?"

"No, they will all have black tips because they are Prime, but their other color is dependent on their parents. I am a Black with black tips because both of my parents were Blacks. It is the highest level of the Prime. I can evolve no further. Nor can my offspring. If a species cannot evolve, they become stagnant."

"So what are you looking for in a mate?"

"That is something only my Dragon knows."

"And he would kill me."

"Yes, for you are small and fragile, and he would not want that in a mate."

"I see." But as she spoke, she felt his cock begin to rise and bump against the back of her thighs. "But it seems you and your Beast do."

"We do, but you have to understand, it is only the Joining Heat."

"Of course it is, because it couldn't have anything to do with me," she said sarcastically. "So what did you do during your other four Joining Heats?"

"I would find a female that was willing to assist me. My Beast never appeared with any of them."

"Well, I guess that's something," she said, rubbing her ass against his growing cock.

"Autumn…" he growled.

"I know. I can feel it too. Where do you need me? Here or on the bed?"

"The bed."

Lifting her up in his arms, he carried her to the bed then carefully laid her down on her back. Ripping away her towel, the gold began to bleed into his eyes as he gazed hungrily down at her. "There is so much I want to do to you. So much of you I want to taste."

"Then do it," she challenged.

# Chapter Five

Kirall lay stretched out on his side, an elbow propping him up as he ran a large hand along her curves. Her skin was so soft and pale that it made her seem even smaller and more fragile as she lay beside him. Her curves weren't as pronounced as they were on the Other females on his planet, but that was the only aspect in which they outshone her.

"You are a truly beautiful creature, Autumn," he told her gruffly.

"Not true, but thank you," she denied, letting her hand slide along his chest. "Is it alright for me to touch you?"

"Yes." Kirall closed his eyes struggling for control as her fingers glided over his chest. Kur, those soft hands had his heat rising, and already he felt the need to spill his seed inside her. But he didn't want this time to be like the ones that had come before, full of only blinding need. This time he wanted to take the time to explore her body, wanted to be as gentle as he could with her.

"What's this?"

Opening his eyes, Kirall looked to what she held so carefully in her hand. "It is called a sleeve. I use it to control my hair so it does not interfere when my Beast emerges."

"But it doesn't interfere with your Dragon?"

"No." He was surprised she would realize that.

"Will you let me see it?" she asked. "Or is that something else not allowed?"

"It is allowed," Kirall told her, reaching down to release the tie that held the sleeve tightly closed.

"Oh. My. God," Autumn gasped when he removed the sleeve and the most amazing mass of thick dark hair suddenly appeared down his back. How had she thought he had short hair. It was so black it was almost iridescent, but along its ends there was a deeper, darker black that for some reason reminded her of the scales she'd seen on his Beast. Reaching out, she found it silky and soft to the touch, not coarse as its thickness had led her to believe. "It's beautiful."

Kirall felt his chest expand, and it wasn't because his Beast was trying to emerge, but because of the swell of pride her words filled him with. Autumn found him attractive. At least he thought that was what she meant until she chuckled softly.

"What do you find so funny?" he growled.

"My dad would have loved to have seen this," she smiled, sliding her fingers through the long strands. "He had hair similar to this.

"Your father had black hair with laminae at the ends?" Kirall couldn't believe it.

"Lamina?" she asked.

"It is similar to my scales only thinner. When I am in my Dragon form, it becomes very hard and sharp, and is used as a weapon against those that get too close."

Autumn carefully touched the ends of his hair, rubbing them between her finger and thumb. It felt as if there was a coating around the ends, not really a scale. It wasn't unpleasant to touch, just different.

"It wasn't like this," she told him. "He had black hair, but his tips were white, like mine. When he was growing up other kids used to tease him about it."

"Why?"

"Because it made him different, made him stand out. Some people aren't very tolerant of those that are different." She gave him a sad smile. "He told me how he used to try cutting the ends off but no matter how short he cut it they always grew back. He even tried to color it, but it would never take. Finally, he just gave up and accepted it."

"He cut off his Laminae!" Kirall roared, sitting up as if shot.

"It wasn't Laminae, Kirall, it was hair." She pushed herself up so she sat on her knees, her butt resting on her heels as she faced him. "I take it that for you, that's a bad thing."

"It is an extreme punishment reserved for only the worst of offenses, for it takes nearly a year for the Laminae to regrow, leaving a Dragon without its protection."

"A year, really?" She reached out to touch the strands he deprived her of when he'd sat up. "Dad would have loved that, me too for that matter. How does it protect your Dragon?"

"The laminae turns into hard, sharp barbs that can be used against any that might attack." Kirall found himself fighting the heat that wanted to overwhelm him as she rubbed her thumb over the points of his laminae. They'd never been sensitive before, but then no female had ever been interested in them either. To distract himself, he asked, "How long did it take your father's to regrow?"

"Dad's never took longer than a day."

"A day!" Kirall reared back in disbelief.

Autumn tightened her grip on his hair stopping him. "Maybe for a dragon and laminae it's different, but my dad wasn't a dragon and his was just hair. Although he always said it was the reason he discovered his one true love."

"Why?" Kirall found himself asking.

"Mom had red hair with white tips, like mine. It was what first drew my dad's attention. When he found out it was natural, that was it for him."

"What do you mean 'natural'?" Kirall frowned.

"Many humans color their hair if they don't like what they were born with. They can put in highlights and streak it with different colors," she quickly explained when she saw his confusion. "Like Kristy had." She waited for him to nod. "Or just do the tips and they can look like this." She held up some of her own hair showing her white ends.

Kirall reached out carefully touching the hair she held, and found the ends very different than his own, softer. "But you do not do this? This is 'natural'?"

"Yes, no self-respecting hair stylist would want to touch this mess," she joked.

"Mess…" Kirall gave her an appalled look. "Your hair is gorgeous, Autumn."

"Yeah, if you like the color of dirt." She gave him a self-deprecating smile. "My parents thought they were being 'inventive' when they named me. We lived in the northeast and the leaves were starting to change when I was born. When they saw my hair, they decided to name me Autumn. I always thought 'dirt' would have been a better description."

"You are wrong," Kirall growled out, "that is not the color of your hair." His fingers sunk deep into the luxurious mass and felt the strands curl around his hand as if they wanted to hold onto him. "This… this is the color of the deepest, darkest of fires. It is full of life and passion. It draws you in, daring you to touch it. Daring you to experience it."

"I… " Autumn found she was speechless at his impassioned words. She'd never thought of her hair in that way before. She'd never really liked the multi-colored strands that had gotten her teased, just like her father. But Kirall's words had her reassessing them. She had always liked her parent's hair and even Jack's, whose was identical to their father's. It was something that had always bound them together as a family, this shared difference.

"Your parents were very wise, Autumn." He frowned when she gave him a sad smile. "Why does saying that make you sad?"

"Because they are gone." Forcing herself to shake off the sadness that always filled her when she thought about her family, she rose up on her knees. She tucked the long strands of Kirall's hair behind his ears, and looked at him for the first time without any fear or anger.

∞ ∞ ∞ ∞ ∞

He was really quite handsome, despite him not being human. The features she'd thought so exotic, if slightly strange when she'd first seen him, now seemed right for him, especially when he was in his Beast form where they were perfectly proportioned. She also realized that with his hair pulled back in the sleeve, the tips of his ears had been covered. Leaning in closer, she saw they were flatter to his head than hers, and came to a point instead of being rounded. Reaching out, she carefully touched a tip and found it was also slightly harder than hers, like his laminae. Following its curve, her fingers ran along his strong jaw. Enjoying the feel of his skin, she let her fingers continue to dance along it, stopping only when she reached his lips.

They were as soft and giving as she'd expected. As she slowly traced them, a sudden need filled her, a need to press her lips against his and give him *her* breath, but she wouldn't. She wouldn't take what was meant for his mate.

Her eyes shot up to his when those lips suddenly opened and captured her finger, sucking it deep into his mouth.

"I thought..." she stuttered as his tongue wrapped around her finger, stroking it the way her channel did his cock. Her channel spasmed in response, and slowly she began to move her finger in and out of his mouth, feeling him grip and release it.

Autumn couldn't believe how erotic it was to watch her finger disappearing into his mouth. Would it be as arousing to watch his cock disappear into her? The thought had her breath shortening and her body flooding with need. Unable to stop herself, she leaned forward and lightly bit his strong chin, watching as gold flared brightly in his eyes.

With her finger still a willing prisoner of his mouth, she let her lips move along the thick vein of his neck, her lips latching onto it. She needed to kiss him, and if she couldn't kiss his lips, then she would kiss him everywhere else.

Running her tongue along the pulsing vein, she gently sucked on it, enjoying his sweet spicy flavor. It was something she knew she could easily become addicted to. Reaching that spot at the base of his neck where he indicated he would bite his mate, she bit slightly and felt him tense.

"Autumn," Kirall relinquished her finger to warn. "You are playing with fire. My Beast..."

"Will never harm me," she told him confidently, knowing in her soul it was true. Neither he nor his Beast was anything like those that had attacked her and her family. Kirall, for all his roughness, for all his gruffness, hadn't truly hurt her. Yes, she had a few bruises, but with her pale skin she always bruised easily, and she could live with that. What she was suddenly discovering she couldn't live without was Kirall.

Pressing her hands against his massive shoulders, she pushed. As he fell back, she straddled his waist. She knew the only reason she was able to do so was because Kirall allowed it. Still, she gave him a triumphant smile.

"Now I have you just where I want you," she teased with a mock 'Beast' growl.

"You think?" Kirall asked, his lips quirking slightly.

"Oh yes." Her smile broadened as her eyes traveled over the feast laid out before her. "It's my turn to wreck havoc on your body, Kirall."

"You think you can?" he challenged even as his cock jerked in anticipation.

"Oh yes, and by the time I'm through with you, the story you tell about your time with me will outshine any told about Kristy."

Autumn wasn't sure where this was coming from. This need to make sure Kirall remembered her. Suddenly she wanted Kirall to be envied for having been allowed to hear her sounds. The way they all did Dacke with Kristy. It was like a tiny ember someone had suddenly breathed life onto deep inside her, and it was growing.

"For that to happen, Autumn, you will have to give me your sounds." Kirall lifted his hips, and his Beast howled his displeasure that his cock was sliding along the hot slick lips that guarded her lair, instead of thrusting into her tight folds.

"If you earn them, Kirall, then I will give them to you. But first," she dug her nails into his chest when he tried to rise, "you will give me your sounds."

"You think you can demand…"

"Yes," she interrupted him. "Whatever you demand from me, Kirall, I will demand from you. Unless you don't think you can handle it."

Kirall and his Beast both growled their displeasure while at the same time they were excited by her challenge. They all knew he was stronger than her, more experienced, and that he had more control, but for her to fearlessly challenge him…

"Do your worst, little Aud-um," he taunted reverting back to his original pronunciation, "and then I will do mine. And I *will* have your sounds."

Autumn just quirked a brow at him, then arching her back she slowly lowered her chest so just the very tips of her breasts touched him. Continuing to move ever so slowly, she stretched out, running them up his body until they were suspended on either side of his mouth, tempting him.

When Kirall's head suddenly lurched up, trying to capture a nipple, she pulled back laughing.

"Oh no, Kirall." She waggled a finger in his face. "It's not going to be that easy for you."

Leaning down, she pressed her lips to his chest, working her way between his flexing pecs until she reached the bounty that lay below. She'd seen Kirall's ripped abs before, had even touched them, but this close she realized she'd never truly appreciated them. Each was like it's own mountain range with high, hard peaks and deep, carved out valleys between them. And while they decreased in length the farther down she traveled, their hardness didn't.

Kirall couldn't believe how amazing it felt to have Autumn's mouth on him.

Her kiss.

The drag of her tongue.

Even the occasional small bite she gave him as she traveled down his body aroused him. But nothing compared to what the scent of her desire was doing to him. It called to him so deeply, and in a way he didn't understand that even his Dragon took notice.

Autumn slid her body further down Kirall's legs, trapping them as she kissed and licked his lower abs, then something

71

nudged her cheek. Turning her head, she found Kirall's cock just a breath away from her mouth.

For a moment she hesitated, but then the molten desire that had been building inside her rose, burning through her insecurities, and she daringly ran her tongue along his slit before fearlessly taking him in her mouth.

"Kur!" Kirall's hips surged up, nearly bucking her off him as her hot mouth ate his cock. Sinking his hands into her hair, he held her in place. He never anticipated she would take him in her mouth, not with her inexperience. He thought she would only stroke him with those soft hands of hers. He knew he could handle that. But this... this was so much more. Groaning, he struggled for control.

Autumn had never given a man a blowjob before. She never had the chance or the desire to, but with Kirall the desire was overwhelming. The sight of that large, pearly drop of pre-cum leaking from his slit was what did it. She needed to taste him, and that small sample of his hot, spicy seed would never satisfy her. She wanted the whole meal, and she was going to have it.

Rising up, her mouth still around his cock, she tightened her legs that were now around his lower thighs keeping him from dislodging her. Then, fisting the base of his cock, she began to consume him.

She started with small, delicious bites, twisting and sucking the bulbous head until she was rewarded with more seed.

"Take more!" Kirall demanded as the hands gripping her hair tightened, moving her up and down the way he wanted.

Autumn willingly complied.

"That's it! Kur, Autumn!"

Never in her life had Autumn felt so powerful. Kirall could easily harm her, kill her, but instead he trembled beneath her, filled with need and desire because of her actions.

Looking up at him through her eyelashes, she found he was using his powerful abs to pull himself up so he could watch his cock disappearing into her mouth. Gold was filling his eyes, and she knew his Beast was close and she wanted him closer.

Biting down lightly, she let her teeth graze his entire length. His hips thrust up in response, choking her while his hands tightened painfully in her hair, holding her in place. Gold nearly consumed his eyes.

"You wish to play with me, little Aud-um?" The rough question came from his Beast. "Then we will play."

Autumn's eyes widened as Kirall's cock began to thicken, growing wider and longer in her mouth and she realized it was because of his Beast's presence. She'd asked for him, now she was going to get him.

Kirall kept his gaze locked on hers as he slowly fed her more of his cock until he reached the back of her throat, and she hadn't even taken half.

"Take more," he ordered.

Autumn found she had no desire to disobey him. Relaxing her throat, Kirall began to fuck her mouth with strong but careful strokes.

"Now swallow!" he demanded, his cock deeply embedded in her throat.

When she did, they both groaned at how amazing it felt.

Kirall pulled back so she could breathe then thrust deeper.

"Again!"

The order was unnecessary as Autumn already was.

"That's it, Autumn," his Beast growled, and she felt the slightest scrape of his claws along her scalp as they extended. "Take it! Take me! Take my seed!"

Autumn's gazed remained locked with Kirall and his Beast's, as with one final thrust he roared, and she greedily accepted the seed that exploded down her throat.

∞ ∞ ∞ ∞ ∞

Autumn gasped when before she even had time to catch her breath, she was flat on her back with Kirall's face inches from hers.

"Kirall!" She looked at him with wide eyes.

"It's my turn now," he told her, and she saw his Beast retreating until gold only rimmed the slightest sliver of Kirall's eyes.

He grasped her wrists in one hand pulling them over her head, stretching her body out as he threw a leg over hers, pinning her to the bed. This stubborn little female had called his Beast, had been able to control him, when he couldn't. It shouldn't have been possible. Only a Dragoon more powerful than him should be able to call his Beast, and there was no one more powerful than Kirall. He was a Black Dragoon. His Beast was a Black Battle Beast.

His gaze roamed down her, and he found the Heat that should have been cooled by her mouth flaring back to life, burning through his still hard cock.

He wanted her this time, wanted his cock to feel those hot, tight walls squeezing it the way her throat had.

"You can't possibly have recovered already," Autumn whispered in amazement and excitement.

"Oh, little Aud-um, you do not know what you have unleashed." He ran a finger along the soft, sensitive skin on one of her raised arms, pausing when he found a long thin scar.

"Don't ask," she told him when he gave her a questioning look.

Kirall knew he would have to get her to tell him before their time was over, otherwise it would haunt him for the rest of his existence. But that was for later. For right now, he needed to hear her sounds of pleasure.

His finger continued its journey down her arm, feeling the shiver that ran through her, then traced her lips that were flushed and swollen from pleasuring him. "You may have satisfied my Beast, but you have yet to satisfy me, and I will be much more demanding."

"Bring it on," she challenged, desire flowing through her along with just a sliver of trepidation. Refusing to let him see it, she captured his finger with her mouth, but instead of sucking it, as she knew he expected, she bit down hard enough to leave a mark.

"You will pay for that, little Aud-um, with screams of pleasure," he promised, pulling his finger away.

"Promises, promises," she couldn't keep from taunting.

"I always keep my promises," he growled, then lowering his head he attacked her neck. He hadn't been able to stop his Beast from emerging after she raked her teeth over his cock, but now his Beast was satisfied and content to stay in the background, and watch as Kirall satisfied Autumn.

"Oh," Autumn couldn't stop the cry from escaping as he sucked at the juncture of her neck. It had her toes curling and her channel flooding with need even as she struggled to free her hands.

"That's it," he growled against her skin. "Give me your sounds, Autumn."

"More," she countered. "Give me more."

Kirall snarled at her challenge, and pulled his mouth away to glare down at her. "Be careful what you ask for, Autumn."

"I'm only asking for you, Kirall."

Kirall couldn't express what her words did to him. He knew she wasn't referring to him in just his Other form, but also to his Beast, and to his Dragon. Never had a female expressed that to him before. It caused his Heat to burn even hotter and made him want to bite her, to mark her as his.

Instead, he ran his hand down her body stopping only long enough to tease each breast by squeezing, pinching, and pulling on each nipple, leaving them as achy and needing as he had been when they'd grazed his chest. Reaching the already soaked curls that guarded her nest, he played with them moving closer and closer to her clit, but never quite touching it.

"Kirall!" Autumn cried out in frustration, trying to move her hips so she could get him to touch her where she needed him to.

"Oh no, Autumn," his finger stayed but a hair's breadth away from her clit. "This time *I* control the pleasure."

"Then give me some!" she all but screamed.

"You are a demanding little Other, aren't you?" Kirall found he liked that, that she was willing to tell him what she wanted instead of just accepting what he gave. "Tell me what you want."

"My clit! Please touch it. I need... Oh!" She found she couldn't speak as his rough finger did exactly as she asked, but only for a single firm stroke. "Kirall!"

"I gave you what you wanted, Autumn." His lips smirked slightly as he looked down at her flushed face. "Was it not enough?"

"You know it wasn't!" Even though her arms were secured over her head and her legs were trapped by one of his, she still glared at him.

"Then tell me what you want. I want to hear it." He lowered his face so close to hers that for a moment she thought he was going to kiss her.

"I want to hear what you want, Autumn. Want to hear what you need, and then I want to hear your pleasure when I give it to you."

"But I..." she slammed her mouth shut.

Kirall pulled back slightly, frowning down at her. Where had his demanding, challenging female suddenly gone?

"But you what?" he asked gently, nearly cooing as he refused to let her break eye contact. "Tell me, Autumn."

"I don't know how to... tell you that is... I've never... only with you."

Kirall's Heat flared at her words. She had been an innocent until him. It was something he kept forgetting because of her fearlessness. The sounds she had given him so far were honest and true, satisfying him even while they increased his desire, but she needed his guidance if he wanted more, for both of them.

"Do you want me to play with your clit?" He watched her eyes flare with desire as he spoke. "To rub and caress it until it is so swollen with need that it feels like it will burst?"

"Yes," she immediately replied breathlessly.

"Then you shall have it, little one." He began to circle her clit again, teasing it with first light then firmer strokes with each pass.

Autumn let out a moan, her hips moving, chasing his finger to keep it on her clit.

"That's it, Autumn," he rewarded her moan by stroking her clit, "let me hear your pleasure."

Autumn writhed under Kirall's touch feeling every muscle in her body tightening as he stroked her clit faster and faster. Her breasts ached and her back arched up offering them to Kirall.

"Should I suckle them, Autumn?" he asked gruffly. "Should I take them as deep into my mouth as you did my cock?"

"God, yes!" she cried out, then closed her eyes, crying out again when he did just that. God, nothing had ever felt as good as him consuming her breast, as feeling him sucking and nipping at it. Her womb clenched in response and heat filled her entire body. She was so close she just needed... something.

Kirall could scent her growing passion, could feel it in the way her entire body tightened, searching for release. Lifting his mouth, he heard her cry out in protest.

"Kirall!"

"Look at me, Autumn!" he ordered.

Kirall's order, along with his hot breath flowing over her wet nipple, had her eyes flying open to be captured by his.

"You will give me your pleasure, Autumn, and you will give it to me now!" With that final order he used the points of his teeth and bit down on the turgid tip of her nipple.

That small bit of pain was all that Autumn needed, and all the tension that had been building in her body released. "Kirall!" she cried out.

∞ ∞ ∞ ∞ ∞

Kirall heard his Beast howl his approval as Autumn cried out her pleasure. It was the first she had willingly given them, and while it satisfied his Beast, Kirall's cock was still filled with heat.

Rolling on top of her, he braced himself up on one arm. Fitting his hips between her legs, he set his cock at her entrance.

"Autumn..." he growled, taking in her pleasure-flushed skin, swollen lips, and the reddened tips of her heaving breasts. She was the very image of a satisfied female. Slowly she raised her thick lashes revealing slumberous eyes.

"I'm not done with you yet." He felt a deep satisfaction as those eyes widened, then immediately filled with desire, as his cock nudged her nest.

"Yes, Kirall," she begged eagerly.

Kirall wanted to howl at her ready acceptance. Not releasing her gaze, he slowly pushed inside her still pulsating channel, wondering how he'd held off for so long. Her channel was so slick from her release, so hot that it drove his heat even higher.

Once she had taken all of him, he began to thrust with... deep... hard... thrusts that had her crying out with pleasure.

"Yes, Kirall. More."

Her breathless demands had him thrusting even deeper, hitting that spot that had her crying out, and her legs wrapped around his hips.

"Kirall." This time the pleading in her voice had him pausing to frown at her. "I want to touch you."

"Then do it!" he ordered gruffly.

"You have my hands," she reminded him pulling down on her arms.

Kirall felt the tug and looked up, surprised to find he still restrained her. He hadn't realized...

The moment Kirall's grip eased, she sunk her hands into his hair and pulled his face down so they were nose-to-nose.

"Now fuck me!" she ordered. "Make me come again."

"Oh, little Aud-um," he growled, starting to thrust again, harder and deeper, "you are in so much trouble now."

Never in his life had Kirall been so challenged. Never had he been so determined to meet that challenge and then surpass it.

The feel of Autumn's hands in his hair, of her nails scraping his scalp... It had his arms sliding under her, supporting his weight as his hands gripped her shoulders, pulling her down to meet his thrusting hips.

Autumn was lost in a haze of pleasure. Never had anyone wanted her like this, needed her like this. She had been alone for so long... had been so cold, but now Kirall was filling her with heat, helping her come back to life, and even if it were only for a day she would take it. She would take all of it.

The orgasm broke over her without warning when Kirall thrust against that spot deep inside her then twisted his hips.

"Kirall!" she cried out, her head tipping back as her nails dug deeper into his scalp.

Kirall felt like the God, Kur, as Autumn cried out his name, her channel clamping down on him. But he wanted more, wanted it for her, wanted it for him, and he would have it!

Refusing to let her demanding channel pull his release from him, Kirall shifted his position. Bracing himself on his hands, he continued thrusting, driving her even higher.

"Kirall!"

"More, Autumn! Give me more!" he demanded continuing to plunge in and out of her channel, sweat streaming down his back. He needed to give her more pleasure than she'd ever experienced. He needed to prove to her that he could. That he was worthy of her sounds.

Autumn couldn't believe the raw ecstasy flooding her body at the new position and felt another orgasm building. Tightening her legs around him, her nails dug into his shoulders, searching for her release.

"Yes, Kirall! That's it! More! I'm so close!"

With each exclamation, Kirall hit that spot, and Autumn was sure her eyes were rolling back in her head.

Kirall could feel his balls tightening, pulling up tight against his body, and knew he wouldn't be able to hold off his release this time.

"Now, Autumn!" he ordered. "Come again now!"

The climax that tore through Autumn was so brutal that it stole her breath, and all she could do was whimper as her body seized.

With one final deep thrust, Kirall's release exploded from him, leaving him so weak in its aftermath that he barely remembered to roll onto his back so he didn't crush Autumn as his cock swelled.

# Chapter Six

When Autumn finally came back to herself, she found she was lying half on and half off Kirall. A leg intertwined with his as she listened to the beat of his heart that had finally steadied, her hand absently caressing his chest. Never in her life had she believed she would ever experience anything like that. It went beyond words, and she knew she was forever changed.

"I understand now," she murmured.

"Understand what?" Kirall asked, just as quietly. He'd wrapped his arms around Autumn when he'd rolled and now he couldn't make himself release her, even though the swelling in his cock had gone down, and he had slipped out of her. He wanted to keep her close, needed to for some reason. One of his hands played with the ends of her hair, while the other made small circles along her hip.

"Why we're not allowed to remember." She lifted her head propping her chin up on his chest so she could look at him. "There's no way a human male could ever compete with that."

Kirall's hands stilled at the thought of her even thinking about joining with a human male. Both his Beast and Dragon agreed and growled loudly at the thought. She was theirs.

But was she?

If the Healer was able to alter her memories, even though she hadn't taken the bolus, then he would have to let her go. But if he couldn't, what was he going to do?

*'Take her with them!'* came the immediate answer from his Beast and Dragon, and he could. She was similar enough to an Other that she could survive on his planet. She could stay in his home, high up in the Papier Mountains, where he could protect and care for her. He would have a fight on his hands for taking her, but he would win because his Autumn was worth it.

Would she be willing to go? Or would she want to stay here, surrounded by all she knew? He needed to find out, but how without letting her know what he was considering? Her next words gave him the chance to find out.

"Will you tell me more about you and your world?" she asked.

He didn't immediately answer, wanting to give the impression he needed to think about it, when inside he was thanking Kur. "Only if you tell me about you and your world."

Her eyes turned serious as they looked at him and he could see she was carefully thinking over her answer.

"Alright, I guess that's fair."

Kirall wanted to roar his success, but he should have known his little Aud-um wouldn't make it that easy.

"But nothing concerning my scars," she added.

"But..."

"No, Kirall, everything else but that. I... I just can't. It hurts too much to talk about. Okay?"

Kirall gazed deep into her eyes, wanting to argue, but what he saw there... such sadness... such pain... and even... fear, had him realizing that this was about more than just what had harmed her. He would eventually find out. He had to, but she needed to tell him willingly.

"Alright," he slowly agreed, "but if you decide you wish to tell me, I will listen."

"Not going to happen, but thank you," she told him with a grateful smile.

"So what do you wish to know?" he asked.

"Tell me more about where you are from," she started. "What did you call it?"

"My world is called Mondu, but my home is high in the Papier mountain range."

"Don't you get lonely?"

"I enjoy my solitude, especially after living my first hundred years in my parents' home."

"I don't understand."

"Only mated pairs can have offspring. Since my parents found each other later in their lives than most, they felt they needed to have as many young as they could, as quickly as they could."

"How many?"

"Seven in just over one hundred years."

"Seven in a hundred years. That doesn't seem quick to me."

"That is because you don't know Dragoons. Most only have offspring once every fifty to one hundred years, because until a young Dragoon is able to shift into their Dragon form, they are vulnerable to attack and must be fiercely protected by their parents."

"When are they able to shift?"

"Not until their fiftieth year."

"I see, so your parents had seven."

"Yes. I am the oldest."

"And you lived with your parents until you were one hundred?"

"Yes. A Dragoon is not allowed to leave his parents' home until he is considered fully grown and able to survive on his own."

"And that happens when?"

"When he has gone through his first Heat."

"At one hundred years."

"Around that time, yes. Many will still stay with their parents long past that, but I found my brothers and sisters very irritating and left as soon as I could."

"That's terrible!" She pushed up and away from him. "You should appreciate your family! What if they were suddenly taken from you?" Her words came out harsher than she intended.

"I do appreciate them," he sat up too, surprised at the intensity of her words. "I only moved to the next mountain range over, Autumn, so I could be close in case my father ever needed my help in protecting them. But I could no longer live there with all the disarray they created."

"Disarray?"

"Yes. Young Dragoons are always testing themselves when they acquire a new skill. After their first shift, they are not always able to control their fire. My brother, Zeb, routinely sent out bursts of it whenever he laughed. One set my sister, Nixie's, hair on fire, and she nearly burnt the house down around us as she chased him, spitting fire the whole way. Zeb was lucky father was there to stop her from incinerating him."

Autumn found herself laughing at the image his words painted.

"It's not funny," Kirall tried to sound harsh, but couldn't contain his smile. "It was always something like that. So as soon as I could, I established my own home. Now, tell me about where you live."

"Me?" Autumn's humor fled. "I live in an apartment with Kristy. You already know that."

"Yes, but why? Why do you live with Kristy and not your family? You are far too young to be on your own."

"Not by human standards," she told him flatly, "and I don't live with my family because they're gone."

"All of them?" Kirall couldn't believe it. For even as irritating as his brothers and sisters could be, he couldn't imagine his life without them.

"Yes. Mom and Dad were both only children. Their parents had also passed on. So, no, I no longer have any family."

"I'm sorry, Autumn. As irritating as my family can sometimes be, I do treasure them."

"I hope you do, because to lose them..." Autumn felt her throat start to tighten, and she knew she couldn't go on; so she changed the subject. "Tell me more about the Dragoon world you rule."

"I do not 'rule' Mondu," Kirall denied. "We have a Council of Elders, of which my father is a member. They solve any disputes that arise in our world."

"But you said you were the highest of the Primes."

"I am, but so are my father, mother, brothers, and sisters. Being the highest of the Primes only means that there are no Dragoons more powerful than us."

"Tell me more, please..."

Looking into her green eyes, Kirall was quickly discovering he could refuse her little, but he didn't know what to tell her.

Autumn watched Kirall struggle with what to say, and realized if she wanted her questions answered, she needed to ask them.

"You said that all Primes, no matter their color, have black tips at the ends of their hair and on their scales." Reaching out, she touched his hair. "That it's a way for others to know their position."

"That is correct," Kirall agreed.

"So what color tips do the Minor Dragoon's have?"

"All Minors have white tips."

"And the Supremes?"

"The Supremes all had silver tips." Kirall brought several of her white tips up rubbing them against his cheek.

"But otherwise, they have the same color hierarchy as you?"

"Yes and no," he told her absently, still playing with her hair.

"What does that mean?" she asked.

"Minors only come in five different colors, the highest being the Whites. There are six for the Primes; the Blacks being a level higher than the Whites. But with the Supremes, there were two more colors above the Blacks. The Reds and the Silvers."

"With the full Silvers being like you, but only in silver."

"Yes, and the Reds would be between the Blacks and the Silvers."

"And Others are below all of those." She found she was beginning to understand.

"Of course, for they are not Dragoons."

Autumn was silent for several minutes, processing everything he had told her then wondered. "So what color was that Supreme that left? Razeth?"

"Razeth was a Red," Kirall told her.

"So what would happen if he returned?" she asked.

"There is little chance of that ever happening, Autumn."

"Why?"

"Because the oldest living Dragoon is now over eight thousand years old, and Razeth was gone long before his birth.

"What about his offspring, if he did find his mate. What if they returned? Would they be welcomed?"

Kirall hesitated before he answered. "I do not know, but the Supremes' power has all but faded from Mondu. It now only remains in Kruba, the home and lands that Razeth once protected. It is the highest and most coveted mountain range on the entire planet, and no one has been able to live there since he left."

"Power. What do you mean?"

"My turn," he told her. "What happened to your family?"

Autumn jerked back in surprise. "I told you that was off-limits."

"No, you did not." Kirall put his arms around her, pulling her back so they were face-to-face. "You only said questions about your scars were off-limits."

Autumn looked up at him unhappily. He was right, but the two were so intertwined...

"You said your father had black hair with white laminae," he prompted.

"Ends, not laminae," she corrected, unable to stop herself from reaching out to touch his that were falling across his chest.

"But you said they were white."

"Yes, so were my mom's and my brother, Jack's. We all had the same strange, white tips."

"You have a brother?" He didn't try to hide his shock.

"Had. Had a brother," she told him stiffly. "He died with my parents."

"I'm sorry, Autumn."

"So am I." She gave him a weak smile. "I loved him, but he could be such a little pain in the butt. His head was always in the clouds."

"What?" Kirall frowned at her. "I don't understand. Your brother, he could fly in the clouds?"

"No." Kirall's words had her smiling slightly. "Although he would have loved that. It means he was a dreamer, always seeing what things could be instead of what they really were. He found 'treasure' everywhere."

"Treasure?" Kirall felt his Dragon cock its head in interest.

"Yes. We'd go for walks, down a path we took every day, and he'd always find something new and 'special', and have to bring it home. His room was full of his treasures."

"So it wasn't 'real' treasure," Kirall said, disappointed.

"Only to Jack."

"So he hoarded it."

"I never thought about it that way, but yes, he did."

"He sounds just like a Dragoon."

"Really? You hoard things?"

"Of course." Kirall gave her a look as if she'd insulted him. "My treasures are protected in my home."

"By your 'power'?"

"Yes." When she just raised an eyebrow at him, he knew they were back to her question.

"Dragoons infuse the territory they protect with their power. It is another way for a lesser Dragoon to know he has trod too far."

"But..."

"Listen, and I will explain it to you the best I can." Kirall waited for her nod before continuing. "The treasure a Dragoon hoards is part of his power. If he loses treasure, his power decreases, and so then does his ability to defend the Others under his protection. When a Dragoon knows he will be away from his treasure for an extended period of time, he can increase that power by having it tap directly into his treasure. The bigger the hoard, the stronger and longer the power will last. Razeth's hoard must have been extremely large to still be able to protect what was once his."

"You protected your home this way? So no one could get in?" Autumn found herself fighting to keep her eyes open.

"I have. Only my direct family members can penetrate the protection I have put in place."

"And Razeth had no direct family members left?" Autumn asked, blinking heavily.

"No, they are gone."

"What happened to the Others that served him?"

"Razeth sent them away before he left. It was as if he knew he would never return." Kirall could see the fatigue his Autumn was fighting. "Rest, Autumn."

"No!" She snapped her eyes open. "I don't like to sleep."

Kirall frowned at her. That was not natural or healthy. A being, every being, needed to sleep. "Why don't you like to sleep?"

"Because then the nightmares will come." Autumn couldn't believe she'd confessed that, and tried to distract him. "Your turn. Ask."

Kirall knew what she was doing. Shifting, he lay back and repositioned her so he could wrap her in the security of his arms. She seemed to need that. His mind was blank, even though it had been filled with questions. He said the first thing that came to mind.

"Why couldn't you go to 'regular' school?" The minute the words were out of his mouth, he knew they were the wrong ones when she stiffened. "Autumn…"

"I was in a hospital. They claimed I was 'ill,' and kept me medicated."

"What?!!" He went to rise, but her soft hand on his chest held him in place.

"It doesn't matter," she told him, unable to believe she'd told him that. Wasn't she the one claiming she didn't want her faults and failures regaled across the universe?

"Autumn…"

"My turn to ask," she quickly changed the subject. "You said your parents found each other late in life. When do Dragoons usually find their mates?"

Kirall let it go for now, knowing it would only upset her if he continued to press. "There is no set timeframe, but it is said that if one does not find a mate in the first fifteen hundred years of their existence, then it is doubtful they ever will."

"And your parents?"

"My father was close to fifteen hundred years old, my mother one thousand."

"And you are five hundred."

"Four hundred and forty-six!" His immediate correction had her smiling sleepily at him, and he suddenly realized she'd done that on purpose.

"I see that age matters in the universe too."

"Not so much matters, but..."

"But what?"

"But it is said that the longer a Dragoon goes without a mate, the worse the Heat becomes. It's been known to drive many insane, and they must be ended."

"Ended?" Autumn frowned at him.

"Yes, otherwise they lose control and rampage."

"You mean like you said you would do if no female was available?"

"Worse, much worse. The Dragoon..." Kirall found he had to swallow hard.

Autumn's hand moved soothingly over his chest. "It's alright, Kirall. You don't have to tell me if you don't want to."

"You need to know." She did if he were going to take her with him. He covered her hand with his, and gave it a squeeze. "It is nothing like what I told you. A Dragoon, driven insane by his Joining Heat, doesn't just take all the available females. He will kill any that do not satisfy him."

"What?" Her eyes widened in shock.

"It is true," he confessed. "That is why Dacke was so willing to assist me."

"But you aren't even five hundred years old!"

"But my Heat is so unusual, it came on so fast, that no one knew what to expect."

"And Kristy was to be the balm that soothed the Heat."

"Balm. I do not understand that word."

"She was to be the thing that would satisfy you. Since she would be willing, compliant, and vocal."

"Yes." Kirall told her the truth, but could see the pain those words caused reflected in her eyes. "Autumn..." He reached out to cup her cheek.

"No." She pulled away from him. "It's okay. I already knew that." But still it hurt. Again she had been seen as less, as a failure. "I'm tired," she told him rolling so her back was to him, "I think I'll rest now. Thank you for talking to me."

∞ ∞ ∞ ∞ ∞

"What brings you to see me, Dacke?" Healer Talfrin asked, surprised to see the Minor Dragoon entering the room set up as a healing area on this planet. He had just finished inspecting it, making sure it had everything he would need to alter the females' memories of their time spent among them. But it also contained a Healing bed as a precaution, just in case one of the males accidentally injured a female. He'd never had to use it before, but he believed in being prepared.

"The human females," Dacke told him.

"What about them?"

"How many of them did you test?"

"How many? All of them." Talfrin frowned, then demanded. "Why?"

"You're sure?" Dacke continued to question.

"Of course, I'm sure. I have the data right here." Talfrin went to his makeshift office and picked up the tablet that held all the names and each female's specifications. He handed it to Dacke. "As you can see it's completely documented. Twenty-four females. All went through testing and cleared. All were given a bolus."

"I see that, but what I don't see is the name of the female that was delivered to Kirall."

"You mean the female you requested return? Kristy?" Talfrin frowned, he didn't recall seeing that name now that he thought of it. "Did she not arrive?"

"No, another female came in her place, and Bonn took her directly to Kirall."

"He did *what?*" Talfrin exclaimed. "Without having her tested first?!! He knows the rules! They were clearly explained to him."

"Which makes me wonder how many of the others he has been ignoring."

"This female with Kirall. We have to get her away from him before it's too late."

"It already is. They have joined, and Kirall is satisfied with her."

"He is..." Talfrin trailed off. "Are you sure it isn't this Kristy with him?"

"I am sure. As is Kirall."

"So you've seen her?"

"You know better than that, Talfrin. A male Dragoon, especially a Prime, never allows his female to be seen by another male during a Joining Heat."

"So how can you be so certain then?"

Dacke hesitated for a moment, Kirall would not be happy with him for telling Talfrin this, but the Healer needed to know. Talfrin was going to have a problem altering this female's memory.

"Because I could scent her boundary blood," Dacke told him.

"Boundary blood?!!"

"You heard me, Talfrin."

"But... what... How is that even possible?" When Dacke just raised an eyebrow, Talfrin flushed. "I know how it is *possible*, I just don't understand how she could possibly satisfy a Prime male during a Joining Heat, especially one like this one."

"I know and I agree, but Kirall refused to give her up, and vows she is unharmed except for the breaching. I don't know how you are going to erase that when the time comes."

"Neither am I. I will have to research it." Talfrin could see something else was bothering Dacke. He owed this Dragoon a great deal. He was the first Dragoon to arrive on Terceira, Talfrin's home world, and he had instantly recognized that they would be unable to defeat General Terron with only the warriors they had. He had immediately sent out a call for assistance, unconcerned with how it would reflect on him.

Because of that, not only had Terceira been saved, but so had Talfrin's family. He owed this Dragoon a great deal.

"What is bothering you, Dacke?"

"Could there be other females... like the one with Kirall, that we do not know about? And if we don't, and your numbers have always matched, then what happened to them?"

Talfrin suddenly understood Dacke's concern. Dragoons, no matter their color or status, were always very protective of females.

"I do not know if we can ever find out if it has happened before, not unless Bonn tells us."

"Doubtful."

"Agreed, but we can make sure this... what's the female's name?"

Dacke frowned, realizing he did not know. "Kirall never told me."

"Well, we will need to find out after the gathering." Talfrin wasn't stupid enough to interrupt Kirall. "But until we do, I can make sure she is the only one at *this* gathering by doing a wellness check on each female."

"Some of the males are not going to like that."

"Their 'likes' have never concerned me. I was against these gatherings in the first place. A female's memories should never be altered without her consent."

"You know why, Talfrin. This planet isn't ready to accept that there are species other than themselves in the universe."

"Then they should be left alone until they are." Talfrin took the tablet from Dacke's hand. I will begin my investigation. You need to find out what you can from the other males here. They may have information we need."

# Chapter Seven

Kirall stared down at Autumn sleeping in his arms. At first, she had just feigned sleep and he let her. He even reached over and dimmed the lights in the room for the first time. It seemed to have done the trick, because not long after that, she truly did fall asleep.

What had driven her to take such an action after having admitted how much she hated to rest? Had it been his words? Had his telling her the truth hurt her so badly that she would prefer nightmares to him?

No part of him found that acceptable.

But nothing about this Joining was 'acceptable' to him. When his Heat had first hit, all he'd wanted was a female... any female... he hadn't cared who, or where, or how, and now that shamed him. For even during a Heat, a female should always be treated with respect. His father had taught him that.

Looking around the room, his shame grew.

Could a female not feel more disrespected?

Even the sheets they lay on were substandard. He hadn't noticed their roughness until just now, and Autumn's skin was so much more delicate than his.

Had they been at his home on Mondu, he would have laid her down on only the softest of sheets. He would have made sure all her needs and desires were met. Food. Drink. Bathing. He would have showered her with jewels from his hoard. He would have worshipped her.

Instead he was here, in a room meant for one that was easily forgotten. And that would never be his Autumn.

He was a Prime Dragoon. A Black on Black. The most powerful of his kind, and yet when it came to this little Other, he had failed. Not only himself, but more importantly her, and that was unacceptable.

He needed to think about how he was going to proceed. Tightening his arms around her so her back was flush against his chest, he then curled his body around hers. He might not yet know what was causing her nightmares... but he would still protect her the best he could. Closing his eyes, he let himself rest.

∞ ∞ ∞ ∞ ∞

"Autumn, stop teasing your brother."

The words had Autumn turning around, and watching as her father and mother rounded the last curve of the path holding hands.

"Dad, she won't let me see what she's found!" Jack complained, jumping up trying to grab what Autumn was holding over her head.

"That's because it's mine," she told him.

"I only want to see it," Jack whined.

"Yeah, right. First I show it to you then before you know it, it's disappeared into your room never to be seen again."

"Well, it would be safer there." He stuck his little chin out at her.

"Right," she said, disbelievingly.

"Autumn, let him see it,." her mother's soft voice told her.

Slowly, Autumn lowered her arm, but she wouldn't let Jack take it from her.

"Let me see that, Autumn." Their father walked up to them and she grudgingly handed it to him.

"This is smoky citrine quartz," he told them, holding it up to the light of the lowering sun. "A nice sized one too. I wonder how it got here."

He handed it back to Autumn. "Come on, let's get home. It's starting to cool off."

"Dad, can we roast marshmallows around the fire pit tonight?" she asked.

"Oh, I don't know, weren't you just teasing your brother?"

"Yeah, well he deserved it," she told him stubbornly. "He won't stay out of my room."

"Jack," Peter frowned down at his son. "What have we told you about that?"

"I know," Jack gave him an abashed look, "but Autumn always finds the neatest stuff."

"Stay out of your sister's room," Peter told him firmly. "Understand?"

"Yes, Dad," Jack responded, but Autumn knew it was only a matter of time before he would be in her room looking for this crystal.

As a family, they walked down the last of the path and into the meadow where their summer cabin sat waiting for them.

"So, Dad, can we roast marshmallows over the firepit after supper?" she pressed.

"Oh yeah! Can we? That would be so cool!" Jack begged as if it were something he'd never done before.

Autumn just rolled her eyes. Everything was like that with Jack. It didn't matter how many times he'd done something, each time was new and exciting. She had to admit it was one of the things she loved about the little twerp. He made life fun, and when he turned those baby blues of his on their parents, they could never say no. They'd gotten a lot of ice cream out of that look.

"You'll have to bring up more wood from the shed," their father warned. "We used it all last night."

"Cool!" Jack turned to fist bump her, their earlier disagreement forgotten. "I'll help after I go check on my room," he told her then took off running for the cabin.

That was another of Jack's little quirks. He always had to make sure his 'treasures' were where he left them whenever they came home.

"You know that means you'll be gathering the wood by yourself," her mother told her in an amused voice.

"Yeah." They all knew once Jack got into his room, they would have to pry him out of it.

"I'll help you after I take out the garbage," her dad told her.

"Okay." Smiling, Autumn skipped ahead of her parents.

A scream suddenly filled the air, freezing them all for a moment. It was Jack. Her dad was the first to react, reaching the cabin just as Jack came flying out the back door, tears streaming down his face.

"They're gone! They're all gone! Someone stole them!" He launched himself into his dad's arms sobbing.

"Jack," Peter's arms easily caught him, "What are you talking about?"

"My room! Someone's been in my room. All my treasures are gone!"

Peter turned questioning eyes to Autumn.

"It wasn't me, Dad." Autumn knew why he thought it might be. To pay her brother back for sneaking into her room, she would often take his things, and wait to see just how long before he would notice. It never took long. "I swear."

"Autumn wouldn't take *everything*, Dad," Jack quickly came to her defense. "It had to be someone else. Monsters, maybe."

Monsters had become Jack's reason for everything bad that happened lately.

"There are no real monsters, Jack," her mother told him, running a comforting hand over his hair that was so like his father's. "Let's go in and look."

"You stay out here," Peter ordered. "I want to make sure whoever broke in is gone."

"Peter..." Mary gave him a concerned look as she took Jack from him.

"I'll be fine, Mary. Stay here with the kids."

"Mom..." Autumn whispered.

"It will be alright, Autumn. Your father will be fine."

Autumn somehow knew her mother was saying it to reassure herself, as much as Autumn.

Even though it felt like an eternity, it really wasn't that long before her father returned, his face grim.

"I called the sheriff," he told them.

"Someone really broke in and took Jack's things?" Mary asked. "What about the rest of the house?"

"It doesn't look like anything else was touched."

"Peter," setting Jack on his feet, she stepped closer to her husband. "That doesn't make any sense," she said in a low voice.

"I know, but it is what it is." They both turned to see that Jack had backed up into Autumn, who had wrapped her arms protectively around him. Both kids gazed up at them uncertainly. "It will be alright, guys. Nothing was taken that can't be replaced."

"But..." Jack started.

"I'll help you find more treasure, Jack." Autumn turned Jack so he faced her. "Better treasure, and we'll start with this." She held out her crystal to him.

"Really?" He raised hopeful eyes to her. "You'd let me have it?"

"Sure," she shrugged like it wasn't a big deal.

Taking the crystal, Jack wrapped his arms around her waist, giving her a big hug as he looked up at her adoringly. "Thanks, Autumn. I promise I'll stay out of your room from now on."

Supper was a quiet affair that night. The sheriff had come and gone, taking his pictures and telling them he would file a report then they had cleaned Jack's room.

As they cleared the dishes, Autumn looked up to her dad. "Dad, are we still going to roast marshmallows?"

"Autumn, I don't think…" her mom started.

"Of course we are," her dad interrupted, giving his wife a silent look. "I'll help you get the wood."

"Alright," her mother finally agreed giving them all a wobbly smile. "Just be careful."

"We will." Peter gave her a hard kiss. "Come on, kids."

Jack jumped up from the table. "I want to hide my crystal first."

"Alright, but if you forget to come out and help then you don't get a marshmallow," his father warned.

"I won't be long," Jack promised.

∞ ∞ ∞ ∞ ∞

"You're a good big sister, Autumn," her father told her, adding a few more pieces of wood to her outstretched arms. "I know you really liked that crystal."

"He's my little brother." Autumn shrugged her shoulders as if that explained it all. "He was scared. I'm supposed to protect him."

"And you weren't scared?" Peter loaded his own arms with wood, and they walked over to the fire pit in the back yard.

"Maybe a little," she told him honestly, because she was always honest with her dad. "Why would someone do that, Dad?" she asked.

"I don't know, honey, but no one was hurt, and that's what really matters, right? Our family is safe and whole."

"Right," she agreed.

"Peter!" They both turned as her mother stuck her head out the side door. "The garbage?"

"Be right there, honey." He turned back to Autumn. "I'll be right back, baby. Will you be okay?"

"I'll be fine, Dad." She started to stack the wood, then looked back and gave him a sassy grin. "You always said I was braver than any Dragon." That was their ongoing joke. Her dad had become fascinated with Dragon lore ever since his grandfather told him they somehow descended from Dragons. Autumn wished she could have met the man. "So let that thief show back up, I'll use my 'claws' on him." She held up her fingers with her short nails in the imitation of claws.

Peter laughed, "I believe you could. I love you, Autumn."

"I love you too, Dad."

∞ ∞ ∞ ∞ ∞

A terrified scream filled the meadow echoing off the mountains.

Her mother's.

Autumn froze, but her father didn't even hesitate, and sprinted to the side door leading to the kitchen and his wife.

And he thought she was brave.

When her father's roar of rage was quickly followed by one of pain, she broke free from her frozen state and followed him.

What she found was blood, pain, and screams.

"No!!!!" she screamed.

∞ ∞ ∞ ∞ ∞

Autumn's scream tore Kirall from his sleep, and his arms instinctively tightened around her, while both his Beast and Dragon rose up ready to attack.

He found himself struggling to hold her in his protective embrace, as she kicked, bit, and fought to get away.

"Autumn!" He refused to release her. "Stop! It's me! Kirall! You are safe!" His words seemed to finally penetrate her nightmare, and her struggles ceased as quickly as they started.

"Kirall?" she whispered, her body still stiff in his arms.

"I'm here, Autumn," he reassured her. "You are safe. My vow. It was only a nightmare."

"It wasn't," she whispered, but her nails stopped digging into his arms. "It was real."

"Then tell me about it so I can help," he found himself pleading.

"You can't. No one can. They're dead."

"Let me try, Autumn." Carefully he turned her so she faced him. "Tell me what happened."

Autumn looked up into his eyes, and saw more than just his Beast was watching.

"Kirall..." she whispered.

"I know. My Dragon is watching... and listening... tell us, Autumn. "

With a trembling hand, she reached out and touched the corner of his eye, wishing she could touch his Dragon. He suddenly gave a strange cough, and she could see from the widening of Kirall's eyes that it had surprised him as much as it did her.

"Was that...?" she trailed off.

"Yes, it was my Dragon. Tell us, Autumn."

Autumn looked at him for several minutes, unsure what to do. She didn't want him to know everything, but she had to tell him something.

"We were at our summer cabin," she began. "It was tucked away up in the mountains, and had been in my dad's family for generations. We would go for a whole month every summer. We'd hike, bike, and fish in the stream during the day. At night, we'd roast marshmallows over the fire while Dad told the most amazing stories, mostly about Dragons." She gave him a small smile. "It was so perfect."

"Go on," he encouraged when she paused.

"It happened on one of the last nights we were there when I was ten. We'd been out all day, walking the trails. When we got back, we discovered that someone had been in the cabin."

"They were still there?"

"No, but they came back when Dad and I were outside. Mom and Jack were inside. When Mom screamed, Dad ran in."

"And you?"

"I froze, by the time I got in the house, it was too late."

"Autumn..." Kirall didn't like how blank her eyes or how flat her voice had become. From the first moment he'd met her, both had been so full of life.

"There was blood everywhere..." she whispered, not noticing his concern. "On the walls. On the floors..."

"Autumn..." he tried to get her to look at him.

"The sheriff came back and found me barely alive.... He'd forgotten to have Dad sign the report."

"If he hadn't?" Kirall didn't know what a 'sheriff' was, but it didn't matter for he already knew the answer to his question as he ran a light hand over her scars.

"Then I would have died with my family."

"Who was it, Autumn?" he demanded, feeling his Heat rise, but this time it was from anger. "Who attacked your family?"

"Drug-crazed teenagers, at least that's what they told me." She shrugged as if it didn't matter. "They found their bodies later in the woods. It seems they turned on each other."

"But?" Kirall prompted.

"Nothing." She shook her head. "I'm sure they were right. After all, I was just a ten-year-old, traumatized child. What I thought I saw couldn't possibly have been real."

"What did you see, Autumn?" When she tried to turn away, he stopped her. "Tell me."

"You'll think I'm crazy."

She gave him the strangest look then started to laugh. It wasn't a pleasant sound.

"Oh my God! Maybe I am. Look who I'm talking to… a man who can turn into a Beast and says he can turn into a Dragon. Maybe I'm still in that damn hospital and none of this is real."

"Autumn!" Kirall shifted his grip, rising so they sat facing one another, and gave her a hard shake not liking her words. "You are here with me! I'm as real as you are!"

"Then maybe I'm not real…"

"Stop!" Kirall wouldn't let her talk like that. "Tell me!"

"I can't!"

Kirall saw something flash in her eyes before she cut herself off, then she seemed to crumble before his eyes. Pulling her legs up to her chest, she curled into a protective ball.

Neither Kirall, his Beast, nor his Dragon could hide their shock at the waves of pain coming from Autumn. They all wanted it to stop.

# Chapter Eight

Autumn didn't know how long she lay there, her back against Kirall's chest, his arms wrapped securely around her. All she knew was she felt safe, protected, and cared about. It had been so long since she had felt any of those things.

For so long her life had been nothing but a haze filled with pain and confusion. She'd finally been able to fight her way out of it, and she refused to go back.

Kirall was real.

The steady beat of his heart against her back was real.

The arms that held her were real.

If that was true, then maybe what she'd seen was real too.

Was it actually possible?

In those early days after the attack, everyone told her she was projecting. That it was her mind's way of trying to make sense of what was incomprehensible. It was only later, when she refused to change her story, that they decided she was crazy and needed to be medicated.

Kirall would know if she was.

∞ ∞ ∞ ∞ ∞

"It wasn't teenagers with knives," she whispered, knowing Kirall was listening intently. "Knives don't rip out people's throats. Teenagers don't hiss a language I've never heard before."

Kirall stiffened, hearing her words. Hissing? There was only one creature in the universe that hissed its language.

"I went running up the steps and into the kitchen after Dad, but before I could take more than a few steps, my feet flew out from under me. My breath was knocked out of me when I landed, and I could only lay there trying to breathe while something warm and sticky soaked into my clothes. When I finally could, I rolled over and came face-to-face with... Dad. He was just lying there, staring at me. Then he... he blinked at me and his lips moved, but nothing came out because his throat was gone. I scrambled away from him. The man that had protected me all my life, I just left him there. To die. Alone."

"Autumn... " He tried to comfort her, but she didn't seem to hear him.

"I turned to get up. To run away, and that's when I saw Mom. She was slumped over on her side, covered in blood, her throat ripped out just like Dad's. Only minutes before she had been alive asking Dad to take out the garbage. Now she was dead, and I suddenly realized that it was blood that had been soaking through my clothes, blood that was covering my hands."

"Their blood."

"I couldn't get it off. I wanted it off. I turned to run to the bathroom on the other side of the house, and that's when I saw them."

"Saw who?!!" Kirall demanded.

"Monsters," she whispered. "The ones that Jack had been so sure existed. I should have listened to him, but lizards aren't supposed to be able to walk on two feet. They aren't supposed to wear pants or attack and kill people."

"Autumn," Kirall turned her so she was facing him, forcing her to meet his gaze. This couldn't be. She had to be wrong. There was no reason for the Varana to attack and kill her family. "Tell me more. How many were there?"

"Three," she immediately answered. "But it was the big one, the one with all the black straps crisscrossing his back that was in charge."

"Straps... " Kirall's voice trailed off. Straps were a status symbol for the Varana, one strap for every Dragoon they killed.

"They had Jack surrounded, and their hissing sounded as if they were laughing at him. Laughing!" She could feel that powerful rage filling her again. "They had just killed our parents, and there they were, laughing at my terrified little brother. I wasn't going to allow that! I wasn't going to let them do to him what they had done to our parents. He was my brother, and it was my job to protect him. So I jumped on the biggest one's back."

"You did what?!!" Kirall couldn't believe it. Varana could be up to eight feet tall, and she'd only been ten.

"The straps made it easy," she told him. "Once I was up high enough, I started clawing at his eyes, and yelling for Jack to run."

"You clawed at his eyes..." Kirall's mind started to race. General Terron's face was scarred, and he had lost an eye with no one knowing who or how he had been injured.

"Yeah, I figured if he couldn't see Jack, then he couldn't hurt him. I was wrong."

"What do you mean?"

"I wasn't fast enough with my hands. He caught my arm in his mouth, yanking me off his back then threw me across the room leaving Jack defenseless since he hadn't run." She ran a finger over the scars on her arm. "After that, he went after Jack. I can still hear Jack's screams, and the hissing laughter that monster made. I somehow got up, and managed to rip Jack out of his grip with my uninjured arm before he could tear Jack's throat out, but then I slipped, and all three of them were on us. I rolled over, making sure Jack was under me. So they clawed at my back, trying to get me to release him but I wouldn't. One of them even stomped on my left leg, snapping my femur, but I still refused to let go. I wasn't going to fail Jack too."

"Autumn, you were only ten," Kirall said softly.

"I'm not sure why they stopped," she continued, not hearing him. "Don't know why they left, but suddenly they were just gone and it got so quiet. Jack wasn't even crying anymore. He just lay there in my arms, looking up at me with those beautiful, blue eyes of his. They were filled with so much pain and so many questions, but he only asked me one."

"What was it?" Kirall asked.

"Where are Mom and Dad?"

"What did you say?"

"That we would all be together soon." She gave Kirall a watery smile as she spoke. "He gave me this small, beautiful smile, and then just faded away. I kissed his cheek and closed my eyes. I knew I would be with them soon. Instead, I woke up in hell… and I guess it was what I deserved."

"Hell? What is hell?" Kirall demanded.

"A place where people go to be punished after they die."

"But you didn't die!" Kirall all but shouted at her. "And you did nothing that deserved punishment."

"I didn't protect my family!" she shouted back. "The most important people in my life!"

"You were fighting with Varana, Autumn! There was no way you could have protected your family from them. That you were able to survive is unprecedented."

"I…" she began to argue back, then gave him a startled look and whispered. "You believe me?"

"Of course I do." Kirall didn't understand why she thought he wouldn't.

"No one else ever has."

The lost look in her eyes had Kirall's heart breaking. "What did they believe?"

"That it was the teenagers they found, not 'giant lizards' like I kept telling them. They blamed it on all the surgeries I had to have."

"Surgeries?"

"Yeah, they had to put metal rods in my arm and leg because the bones were shattered, and it took multiple surgeries to repair my back. I kept having nightmares. I would wake up screaming and try to run away. They couldn't restrain me on the bed, not with my injuries, so instead they medicated me to the point where I couldn't move or speak."

"They did what?!!" Kirall was outraged at the thought. "How long did they keep you like that?"

"I'm not sure. At least until my back was healed enough so I could lie on it. That's when they started easing me off the meds. But when I continued to insist it was 'giant lizards', and not teenagers, they determined the stress had been too much and I had lost my mind. So they gave me different drugs. Drugs for crazy people. They hurt so much. It felt like they were killing something inside me, something I needed to protect. I wanted to scream for them to stop, but I couldn't."

"These drugs… silenced you?"

"Yes. It was like they created this wall between my mind, my body, and my soul. I couldn't connect anything, couldn't explain anything. I could see and hear, and physically I could eat and swallow, if they put it in my mouth. They forced pills down my throat and every time they did, I'd scream in my mind. Then I'd hear the 'lizards' laughing at me, and I swore I'd never scream again."

Kirall now understood why she was so adamant about controlling her sounds, about not screaming. She associated them with pain and defeat.

"How did you break through?" he asked after several long minutes. "The wall the drugs created."

"I couldn't, I tried and tried, but I always failed."

"Then how are you here?"

"Because my insurance ran out," she told him quietly.

"What? Insurance?"

"It is what paid for all my treatments, for my care. After I maxed out, I became a ward of the state, and was moved to an overfilled, understaffed facility that didn't always hire the most... reputable people. The guy who was supposed to be giving me my meds started stealing them instead, and slowly the walls started to come down."

"So they let you go."

"Not right away. First, I had to convince them that I was 'cured', so I told them what they wanted to hear. That it was crazed teenagers that attacked and killed my family with knives. I was even able to describe the knives because the sheriff and doctors had talked about them when they were in my room, and thought the drugs had knocked me out."

"So they believed you."

"Of course. It's what they wanted to hear, and then there was the fact that it was financially beneficial for them to release me."

"Financially beneficial?"

"It would save them money if I was gone," she told him. "So they discharged me."

"How old... how old were you when they just thrust you out into the world? Abandoning you."

Autumn's eyes widened. Surprised he understood that. She'd been terrified. If not for the help of an amazing social worker, she didn't know what she would have done. "Eighteen," she told him quietly. "I'd just turned eighteen."

Kirall couldn't imagine being on his own at such a young age. He'd been under his parents' protection until his first Heat occurred at one hundred. While he'd sometimes chafed at their restrictions, he'd always known he was safe and protected. Autumn hadn't had that. His anger began to burn at how badly she'd been treated. "And you had no one there to protect you?"

"There was one person, a social worker. She did what she could to help me. She got me into the classes I needed, then found me a place in a homeless shelter where I could stay and get at least one hot meal a day. I was able to get a job at a cafe washing dishes, and eventually moved up to waitressing. It's where I met Kristy, and once I got my G.E.D., I was able to take a second job, move out of the shelter, and in with Kristy."

"How old are you now, Autumn?" Kirall asked quietly.

"Twenty-two." She frowned at him. "Why?"

"You are so young to have survived so much."

"Have I? Survived, that is?" she asked because sometimes she wasn't sure she had, especially when the nightmares came. When that happened, she was thrown back into all that pain and confusion, and found herself having to fight her way back out again.

"You have, Autumn," he told her firmly. "The Varana you attacked is one of their strongest and most-feared males. You injured him, something no one else has ever been able to do."

"You know this... Varana?"

"Yes. He is General Terron. He leads the Varanians, but I don't understand why he would attack you and your family." He slowly lifted a strand of her hair, looking at its unusual white tips. "Unless for some reason he thought you were a Dragoon."

113

"A Dragoon? You mean because of my hair?"

"Yes. The Varana are always trying to expand their territory by eliminating weaker species and taking over their planet. Dragoons are the only ones that can truly defeat them. That is why they attack our young before they are able to shift and protect themselves. They also attack Others that they think might be our mates."

"They are trying to wipe you out by killing your children and mates."

"Yes, but they will not succeed," he told her confidently. "We eradicated them from Terceira, and we will continue to do so, wherever they appear."

"Terceira, that's where you are coming from?"

"Yes. The Varana had taken over the planet, killing most of the inhabitants. It took some time, but we were able to drive them out."

"Just you and Dacke?" She couldn't hide her astonishment.

"No, there were others on Terceira. They are returning home on different ships."

"Was..." Autumn wasn't sure she wanted to know.

"Yes, General Terron was there." He watched her slowly nod, and saw fear filtering through her eyes. "He fled like the coward he is. He will never get near you again, Autumn. Will never be able to harm you. My vow."

"Thank you, but you can't make that vow, Kirall," she told him sadly.

"Of course I can!" He reared back as if she'd struck him.

"No, you can't," she argued, wanting to reach out and touch him, but refusing to let herself. She wasn't going to let him give her false hope that she might be safe, even if it was only for a few hours. "After tomorrow you will be gone. I will return to my life, remembering nothing about our time together, except that it was 'pleasant', and you... you will return to your world, find your mate, and never concern yourself with what might have happened to me."

"That's not true!" Kirall roared, sitting up.

"It is," she sat up too, "and it's okay. The only reason you're here is because of your Joining Heat. You told me that yourself. I survived before you got here. I'll survive once you're gone."

∞ ∞ ∞ ∞ ∞

Kirall found himself struggling to control not only his Beast, but also his Dragon as neither liked what she was saying. Did she really believe they would just go, leaving her unprotected and forget about her?

That was never going to happen.

She had become too important to all of them to let her go.

Just the thought of her forgetting their time together had his Heat rising so fast it overwhelmed him.

"You are no longer alone, Autumn," he growled. Gripping her waist, he pulled her up as he rose to his knees. "We are with you," his Beast told her, gold filling Kirall's eyes.

It should have shocked her, this swift change in him, the feel of his Beast's hands and claws around her waist, but it didn't. What *did* shock her was that his eyes had started to elongate, and suddenly his Dragon was staring directly out at her, his eyes reminding her of the crystal she'd given to Jack so many years ago. Black scales began covering his face and neck, and Kirall's features began to change. His mouth and nose extended while his laminae turned into hard, sharp points.

Slowly, Autumn reached out. She wasn't worried about being bitten, but didn't want to chance it either, for the teeth in Kirall's Dragon's mouth looked deadly sharp. Carefully, she touched his snout. Surprised at how smooth and soft his scales were. They were interlocking, and formed the most amazing, shimmery skin and felt nothing like the fish scales she'd expected.

Moving her fingers up his snout, she traced where one of Kirall's eyebrows should have been. It was now a hard ridge, that went from the inner corner of his eye to the outer corner, seeming to protect it before it disappeared back into his hair.

Smoky, crystal eyes watched her intently, assessing her as she touched the corner of his eye.

"You're beautiful," she whispered, lightly kissing the place where her fingers had been.

Kirall's Dragon coughed softly, and Autumn tipped her head to the side letting his snout brush against her neck. His hot, moist breath caused her to shiver. Not with fear, but with need. When he reached the curve where her neck met her shoulder, his rough tongue swept out, tasting her.

"Autumn..." The deep gruffness of the voice had her twisting her head slightly, and for a moment she saw all three of Kirall's beings in his face before his features settled back into his Other form.

Kirall looked down at Autumn, and for the first time felt his three forms truly become one being. It was what mated pairs said happened when a Dragoon found its mate. Not only did the mated pair become one, but so did all their forms. It was what allowed a mate to ascend to a higher level.

Suddenly it all made sense, and he couldn't believe he hadn't realized it earlier.

The sudden onset of his Heat.

The way she was able to calm his Beast.

The way his Dragon accepted her.

He wasn't in a Joining Heat.

He was in his Mating Heat.

It didn't matter that Autumn was an Other.

She was his mate.

He felt his Heat rising, and knew it was time to fully claim his little Other in the way Dragoons had been doing it since the dawn of creation. Then she would be their mate forever!

Autumn's eyes widened as she watched Kirall. So many emotions were flying across his face that she couldn't tell what he was thinking, let alone feeling. Was he upset that she had touched his Dragon?

"Oh, little Aud-um," he growled, his eyes glowing slightly. "Now you are going to get everything you've been asking for."

Autumn's breath hitched at the dark promise she saw in his eyes, but before she could reply she found herself spun around and on all fours. Kirall's thighs slid between hers, spreading them wide as he settled in behind her. He pressed his chest against her back, his weight supported by his hands on either side of her.

"Do you willingly accept me, little Aud-um?" he asked, moving her hair over to one side so he could lick the same spot his Dragon had and whispered, "In all my forms?"

Autumn found she couldn't answer as Kirall's Heat surrounded her. The feel of his tongue, tracing the same path as his Dragon, had her womb clenching and her channel flooded with need.

"You must say it, Autumn," he told her, lightly raking his teeth over her neck.

"I accept you!" she gasped. "All of you!"

"That's good, little one," he growled, "because I wasn't going to let you refuse me."

With that, Kirall rose up, his hands gently tracing the scars that covered her back. It still enraged him that she had been so

117

severely injured, but he no longer saw her back as damaged. Instead he saw it as a tribute to her deep love for her brother.

"You are so beautiful, little one," he whispered. "So strong." Autumn looked back at him, giving him a disbelieving look. "It is true. You willingly sacrificed yourself trying to protect someone you loved. That you didn't succeed does not matter. You gave everything you had. It is all any of us can do."

Autumn felt her eyes fill at Kirall's words. For so long she believed she was weak and a failure. For Kirall to tell her she was neither touched her deeply. She was about to tell him that, when she felt something move along her hip. She knew it wasn't one of Kirall's hands because she could still feel them on her back.

Looking toward her hip, her eyes widened when she saw something thick and black working its way along it.

"Kirall... is that...?"

"Yes. My Dragon wants to explore you, wants to caress and pleasure you as much as I do. This is the only way he can. He would never harm you, Autumn."

"I know that, it just surprised me." She shivered, then dropped her head between her arms, and watched, feeling his tail lightly caress her stomach. He wrapped around her again before paying attention to each breast, squeezing and teasing them until her nipples ached.

"Oh..." she cried out softly.

"That's it, Autumn," Kirall told her, rubbing his hands over her ass. "Let us hear your sounds of pleasure. That's all we want to give you. Pleasure. Never pain. Never again."

Autumn knew that was true. She felt safe and protected wrapped in the embrace of Kirall's Dragon. Still, she tensed when he brushed against her cheek. She expected the tip to be sharp since it was meant for defense. Instead, it was covered in scales as smooth and soft as the ones she'd touched on his face. She watched in amazement as the scales slowly receded, revealing the deadly-looking spike she'd expected. It was then safely encased back inside the soft, interlocking scales.

She immediately understood. His Dragon was trying to reassure her that his touch wouldn't harm her. "I know," she whispered, knowing he would hear her, and was rewarded by him running his tip along her bottom lip.

She let her tongue slip out of her mouth to run along the covered tip, returning the caress. His bands responded by tightening around her. When he slipped further into her mouth, she welcomed him by closing her lips around him. Behind her, she heard Kirall groan, and realized he was able to feel what his Dragon was feeling, that they were truly one being.

"Yes, Autumn," his hands tightened on her hips, pulling her back so his cock could slide between the cheeks of her ass. He groaned when they squeezed him in return. Reaching around her front, his hand slid into her curls. "You are so wet already, little Autumn. Does it excite you that my Dragon desires you?"

With her mouth full, Autumn could only mumble her answer.

"That he wants to fuck you as much as I do?" He began to stroke her clit in the way he knew she liked. "We are going to, Autumn. But first, you are going to come for us. We are going to show you just how much pleasure we can give you."

Autumn pressed back against him, seeking relief from the need building in her as his fingers strummed faster and faster against her clit. She was so close to coming, but she wanted more. She wanted Kirall's cock deep inside her. Wanted him pounding into her, filling her, the way she knew only he could. But she wasn't willing to give up the treat in her mouth to tell him.

"That's it, Autumn," he encouraged, feeling her body start to tremble. "Come for us. Give us more of your sweet nectar. Coat my fingers with it." He began pressing even harder against her clit. "Give it to us, and we will fill you like you've never been filled before. We will give you what you've been wanting from all of us!" Kirall ground his hips against Autumn, his fingers pinching her clit. His Dragon finally relinquished her mouth, his bands tightening around her keeping her close as her orgasm ripped through her.

It was Kirall's words, the passion behind them, the demand, and the promise that finally sent her over the edge, even while her channel protested that it had nothing inside it.

Autumn's head fell between her arms as she tried to catch her breath. Her body was still trembling from her orgasm, but she wanted more. She felt this deep, burning need, and knew the only thing that would satisfy it was Kirall's cock filling her.

"Kirall..." she pleaded.

"Soon, little one," he promised. "Soon we will give you everything."

"But... Oh!" she gasped. Kirall's finger had moved away from her clit, but now his Dragon was sliding along it, curling around it, coating himself with her slickness.

"Do you like that, little Aud-um?" Kirall whispered. "Do you like how my Dragon touches you? How he wants to absorb your essence so that when he flies high in the sky, every Dragon will scent that you are ours."

"Yes," she said breathlessly.

Kirall pushed back from her hips, leaving a space between them. "You have accepted us, Autumn, and we are going to claim you the way a Dragoon claims an Other."

"What does that..." her words trailed off as she felt Kirall's Dragon move around the outside of her hip before sliding down to where Kirall's cock had just been pressing against the tight rosebud of her ass. "Kirall..."

"Let him in, Autumn," Kirall palmed her cheeks when he felt her tense. "Let him love you."

Autumn remembered how fascinated she had been when she'd found one of Kristy's 'toys' that had been left in the bathroom. It had a tapered tip with ribs that got larger as they got closer to the base. When she finally got up the nerve to ask Kristy what it was, Kristy had laughed, and said it was a butt plug. She'd then gone into great detail about its use, and how amazing it felt.

It made Autumn curious, but not curious enough to get one when Kristy had offered to take her to her favorite 'toy' store, and help her pick one out. Now Autumn was about to experience it for real with Kirall. She found she wanted to, and that she was excited by the thought. Forcing herself to relax, she pushed back slightly and was surprised when the tapered end, slick with her juices, entered her without the pain Kristy had told her to expect.

Slowly he pressed deeper. The tip became wider and thicker, more like the head of a cock. She remembered it had happened when he had been in her mouth too. It felt strange, but was also amazing. She began to move, wanting more... needing more.

"No, little one," Kirall's hands tightened on her hips holding her still. "That is for us to do, to show you how well we can pleasure you. All you need to do is enjoy."

Autumn was about to demand that he do it then when Kirall's grip shifted to her waist. He lifted her up until her back was pressed high against his chest, and the head of his cock nudged her entrance. Her legs swung back, bracing herself against the hard muscles of his upper thighs the best she could. She reached up, her hands clutching the back of his neck.

Slowly, Kirall lowered her onto his cock. Even though she was slick and wet from her release, he had to work to fit his engorged head inside her tight little channel.

"Kirall!" she cried out as he slowly filled her to the hilt. Never could she have imagined something like this. The bands of his Dragon tightened around her, holding her securely in place as Kirall's hands moved, capturing her uplifted breasts, his fingers rolling her nipples.

"We have you, little one," he growled into her hair then slowly began to move his hips, thrusting in and out of her channel as his Dragon did the same in her ass. Never had Kirall felt anything as amazing as his mate clamping around both of them. Accepting them. He felt the claws in his hands extending, and knew his Beast was loving her as much as they were.

Autumn's head fell back to rest on his shoulder as her system was swamped with never before felt sensations, and they weren't all physical.

Yes, she was being physically loved in a way she never had before, but she could also feel the depth of that love coming from every part of him.

It was in the way his Dragon held her so securely, yet so carefully in his embrace.

It was in the way his Beast captured her breasts, letting her feel his deadly claws, but making sure she knew they would never be used against her.

Then there was Kirall himself. Looking up, she saw everything he felt for her in his eyes. His need. His desire. His love.

"Autumn..." he growled softly then lowering his head, he captured her lips giving her something he'd never given another and never would again.

His kiss.

His life's breath.

Autumn's back arched away from his chest, her nails digging into the back of his neck as wave after wave of Kirall's Heat burned through her like a forest fire, stirring up something deep inside her.

Her hips, despite being securely held by his Dragon, tried to pump furiously. She was being consumed by need and desire, and she wanted more. More from all of them.

"Kirall!" she cried out, ripping her mouth from his. "More! Please! Harder! I need you! All of you!" She heard his Beast growl, and felt his cock expand her channel to its very limits as he thrust harder and deeper, giving her what she demanded.

She watched as Kirall's features began to shift. First, his Beast appeared, and with his shorter snout nudged her head to the side. She kept her gaze on him, her channel clenching with need as his tongue bathed the juncture of her neck and shoulder.

Then his Dragon took over, watching her with his crystalline eyes as his lips slowly pulled back to reveal his razor-sharp teeth. Before she could feel even a hint of fear, he struck, his teeth sinking deep into the giving flesh and forever marking her as theirs.

Autumn's entire body seized as he took her blood, mixed it with his own then injected it back into her. His kiss had burned, but this... this was something else. It was like lava bubbling through her veins, incinerating her as it looked for that special place to erupt. When it reached her womb, it did just that.

"Kirall!" she screamed out in pleasure as her orgasm exploded through her, awakening all she'd been forced to suppress.

Kirall roared as Autumn's body clutched around him, and she screamed out her pleasure for all to hear. He thrust deep one last time, his seed exploding from the very depths of his balls, bathing her womb in its fiery heat. Knowing that this time, there was a chance it could take root.

# Chapter Nine

The changing room was in shambles as Bonn released his rage on it, throwing chairs and flipping over tables.

At 6'2", he was solid muscle, and he was used to intimidating people. He liked being able to, and if his size didn't do it, his money did.

Bonn had a lot of money. All from supplying women for a bunch of aliens to have sex with.

He had accidentally fallen into the job a few years ago when the previous curator had gotten into some trouble at the club that Bonn was the bouncer for. Before Bonn could pound the shit out of him, Neeley had offered him a weekend job that would pay him more than he would make in a year at the club, and all he had to do was check I.D.s.

Bonn quickly discovered what was really going on, and Neeley had to make him his assistant to keep him quiet. Had he been shocked when he learned their clientele were actually aliens? Maybe for a moment, but then most of the 'humans' he worked with were pretty strange too. Now, after Neeley had an unfortunate accident, Bonn was the curator.

Did he care that they were only here to fuck women?

That the women would never know what had been done to them?

Fuck no! Not as long as the money kept coming in.

Now all that was in jeopardy. All because of one fucking woman!

His hands shook with rage as he stared down at the paperwork he'd forgotten in this room.

Kristy Pwff.

5' 7" tall.

Brown hair with red and white highlights.

Blue eyes.

That wasn't anything like the woman he'd escorted to the Dragoon's room!

"You didn't check this?!!" he demanded of Rattler.

"Why would I? She came in the limo you sent! I asked her name. She said she was Kristy Pwff."

"And you didn't take her through testing?!!"

"Why would I? She was a repeat and you ordered me to bring her directly to you."

If the girl had gone to who she was supposed to, none of this would have happened because Dacke would have immediately known she wasn't Kristy. Instead, she'd been taken to someone called Kirall, who was apparently an especially horny alien that everyone seemed to fear.

Bonn didn't care who fucked the girl as long as he got paid, but if what Rattler had overheard was true then that was now in jeopardy. All because of this one girl.

Bonn's hands shredded the paperwork, wishing it was the girl's neck. Why was she here? How was he going to get rid of her?

He had to get her out of that room, and the sooner the better! But how? Apparently, the alien liked her. Which was good. So maybe this wasn't as big a cluster fuck as he thought. He'd just wait until this Kirall was finished with her, let them alter her memories, and that would be it.

If she met with an unfortunate accident after they were gone... well, they'd never know about it, now would they?

Bonn took a calming breath and smiled. Yes, that was it. Everything would be fine. Reaching down, he started picking up the destroyed paperwork that had flown everywhere. That was something else the aliens demanded, that the rooms be immaculately clean at all times.

Moving around the room, his smile disappeared.

What was that?

His eyes narrowed as he moved toward the white object on the floor. It wasn't paper. Reaching down, he picked it up. It was a pill. The bolus he'd given to the girl! When had she spit it out?

Fuck! What was he going to do now?!!

The bolus was how the Healer would start altering the woman's memories. If she didn't take it....

What would they do when they found out?

To him!

He had to get rid of the girl before they found out!

Crushing the pill between his finger and thumb, he looked at Rattler. "Gather the men and meet me outside the room the girl is in."

∞ ∞ ∞ ∞ ∞

Autumn lay on her side, wrapped in Kirall's arms, his Beast and Dragon having receded. Staring at the wall, she tried to put her shattered mind and body back together. What Kirall had just done to her had been...

Amazing... no that was too tame of a word.

Earth shattering... no that was wrong.

Life altering! That was it, because Autumn knew that even with her memories erased, she would never be the same girl she had been before she'd met Kirall. She was forever altered.

Kirall had marked her.

No, wait... he'd bitten her... kissed her....

"Kirall..." she said hesitantly.

"Hmm?" he growled softly, a hand making small circles over her stomach.

127

"You kissed me."

"Yes."

"On the lips," she clarified.

"Yes."

"Why?" She twisted around in his arms.

"Why what?" he asked, grunting his displeasure when his softened cock slid from inside her.

"Why did you kiss me? Bite me. You said those were things you would do only with your mate."

"That is true," he said. His voice filled with great satisfaction.

"Then why did you do them with me?"

"Because you are my mate, Autumn."

"What?!!" she demanded, sitting up.

"I said," Kirall didn't move, just reached up to gently caress his mark on her shoulder. He couldn't explain what it did to him to see it on her. "That you are my mate."

Kirall's touch sent a shiver of desire running through her before his words sank in. "No! That's not possible," she denied, and would have risen from the bed if he hadn't pulled her back into his arms.

"Why is it impossible?" he asked, kissing her lips.

"Because I can't be. You must refuse me!"

"Refuse you?!!" he looked at her in shock.

She saw something flash in his eyes. It couldn't have been hurt… could it?

"Yes!" She wouldn't let herself back down. "You said taking an Other mate weakens a Dragoon, that you can refuse to take an Other, and still be able to find a better, stronger, Dragoon mate!

"Autumn…"

He suddenly began to realize her concern.

"I'm not a Dragoon. I'm not even an Other, and I am already damaged! You are going to be constantly attacked because of me, and I'll be just as useless protecting you as I was with my parents and Jack! I won't go through that again! I won't let your pity for what happened to me get you killed! You must refuse me!"

Kirall's roar caused the walls to shake, and for the first time, Autumn saw him truly enraged.

At her.

"You are not damaged!" He flipped her over onto her back, then leaned down so his face was inches from hers. "Never say that again! You are a survivor! Do you think so little of me that I would turn my back on you because you are not Dragoon?!!"

She watched his face shift as all three of his forms wanted to dominate. She saw the pain it caused him.

"Stop." Unable to stand seeing him in pain, she reached up and touched his cheek. "Please, Kirall… calm."

"How can you ask that of me!" he demanded, still angry, but her touch was able to calm his Beast and Dragon some.

"Kirall…" She fought back the tears that wanted to fill her eyes. She was doing this for him. "Your Joining Heat is confusing you."

"Mating Heat," he immediately corrected. "Autumn," he lowered his forehead to hers as he caught the shimmer of tears in her eyes. "I owe you the deepest of apologies. I should have immediately realized what was happening, but because I did not, you now doubt me."

"It can't be…"

"It can. It is." He brushed his lips against hers, reveling in his right to do so. "I've been told all my life what to expect when my mate first comes near. About how intense the Heat can be, and how suddenly it can come on. I just never realized…"

"It wasn't meant for me, Kirall," she told him, trying not to let him see how that saddened her. "I was just the one here."

"That's not true! You are the only one it was meant for. I know this is all new and confusing for you, Autumn, but you must believe me. Once a Mating Heat starts, only a mate can touch the Dragoon. He or she will kill any other that tries. It is why you are able to calm my Beast. Why my Dragon was so interested in you and joined with you. It is why I kissed you and joined our lives."

"By giving me your life's breath and blood."

"Yes. It will extend your life, and forever tie us together."

"Does it harm you?" she asked.

"No," he gently cupped her cheek. "It may weaken me for a short time while my body adjusts, but that is all."

"You're sure?"

"Yes, little one." Looking at her, Kirall was surprised to find he felt stronger, not weaker now. "The finding of your mate is the most precious gift the God, Kur, can give a Dragoon. I thought I understood that, but I didn't. Not until I met you. You are now my only reason for living. Without you, my life is meaningless."

Autumn felt her eyes start to fill, and this time when he lowered his head, she met him halfway. Her fingers sank deep into his hair as she gripped the back of his head to keep him close. Here was the acceptance she'd been looking for since the attack on her family. Here was the love, and she wasn't going to lose it again.

Kirall settled between thighs that eagerly opened for him, never breaking the kiss. He was going to show his mate just how much he loved her, and he would keep doing it until she believed him.

The sound of the outer door bursting open had Kirall immediately springing to his feet. His Beast emerged, ready to defend their mate against any who dared enter their lair.

Charging into the outer room, he found a half-dozen, puny, human males storming in. His Battle Beast, ready to shred and destroy, roared out his intent.

∞ ∞ ∞ ∞ ∞

Dacke had just finished speaking to the males in the lounge and was on his way to discuss what he had discovered with Talfrin, when he heard the roar of Kirall's Battle Beast. Rounding the corner, he was shocked to find human males storming into Kirall's lair.

Did they have a death wish?

∞ ∞ ∞ ∞ ∞

"Get him!" Bonn ordered from behind his men who had skidded to a halt upon what they were seeing. They were all large men, thugs really, and they were used to easily overpowering everyone. But they'd never gone up against a nine-foot Battle Beast, and they instantly knew they could never defeat him.

∞ ∞ ∞ ∞ ∞

Autumn was staring up at the ceiling, not sure what had just happened. One minute she and Kirall were about to make love again, and the next he was gone. What was going on?

Suddenly, she heard Kirall's enraged roar and everything within her froze, just as it had when the Varana attacked her parents.

*'Kirall!'* Autumn's mind screamed. *'Kirall is crying out for help. He is being attacked!'*

This couldn't be happening again!

She wouldn't let it!

She couldn't survive being left alone again!

She had failed her family. She hadn't been strong enough to protect them. Hadn't dug deep enough to find that part of her that could.

She wasn't going to do that with Kirall. She wasn't going to fail him too. Wasn't going to watch him die.

Breaking through all the barriers that had held her back before, she went to defend her mate.

∞ ∞ ∞ ∞ ∞

"You dare enter my lair!" Kirall growled, his gaze traveling over the males that were quickly trying to retreat. The scent of their fear filled the room as he let his claws extend to their full, deadly length.

"Now you will find out what happens when a Dragoon's mate is threatened." An enraged roar coming from behind him, followed by the sounds of furniture breaking, and metal hitting the floor had Kirall spinning around to find a small, red Dragon charging into the room. Tendrils of smoke escaped flaring nostrils as eyes, as silver as the tips of the scales covering its body, wildly searched the room before settling on him.

It was Autumn! Of course it was! He was truly a stupid male!

She had told him how she had clawed at General Terron's face, trying to protect her brother. He had seen the evidence of

132

that attack himself, but he had never put it all together. Somehow, as a ten-year-old, she had been able to partially shift! It was something he'd never heard of a female Dragoon being able to do. No wonder the Varana had attacked her so viciously. Somehow they had known that Autumn and her family descended from Razeth, and had set out to eliminate them as they were trying to do all the Dragoons.

He should have realized earlier that she couldn't have been an Other.

She openly challenged him, a Black Prime.

She didn't fear either his Beast or his Dragon.

Her fire had burned just as strongly as his when they had kissed. He just hadn't realized it. He also hadn't realized that the extra burn that had filled him when he had mixed their blood wasn't from desire, but because hers was the more powerful blood. His bite wasn't going to change her. He would be the one changing, becoming a Supreme, once her Dragon marked him as her mate.

She was only twenty-two, and she was already able to shift into her Dragon form.

His mate was truly amazing.

And by the looks of it, she was truly pissed!

"Kur! It's a Supreme!"

Dacke's whispered words drew the gaze of Autumn's Dragon, and the smoke she was emitting began to darken.

Seeing it, Kirall quickly moved to stand between the two, shifting back to his Other form, his arms outspread.

"It's alright, Autumn. I am fine." But her eyes continued to look wildly behind him, focusing on the remaining males, her smoke darkening.

"No, Autumn!" He stepped in front of her, his arms spread. "You will incinerate us all! You must calm, my love." He carefully put a hand on her snout, caressing it. "You are so beautiful, Autumn."

She snorted in disbelief, but when her gaze met his again, the wildness in her eyes had begun to retreat, and the green he so loved was starting to return. "Your Dragon is so beautiful, Autumn."

Autumn frowned at Kirall. *Her Dragon? What was he talking about?*

Looking down, she discovered that instead of the normal skin and hands she was used to seeing, there were now scale-covered limbs with long, sharp claws. Her startled gaze shot back to Kirall.

Kirall saw the fear and confusion in her eyes, and realized she hadn't known she'd called her Dragon. She probably didn't even realize she had partially shifted when she tried to protect her brother.

"It is alright, Autumn," he told her. "Just shift back." The panic filled gaze that met his made him realize she didn't know how.

"It is alright, my Autumn," he cooed to her, "just imagine yourself as you were." He ran a soothing hand along her long neck as he spoke. "With your long, red hair and those flashing, green eyes. I'll be right here with you."

He felt her large head settle on his shoulder as a shudder overtook her. One minute he was holding a beautiful Dragon in his arms, and the next his very beautiful and very naked mate. She lifted her head, smiling up at him when suddenly her face contorted, and the most horrific pain-filled scream he had ever heard filled the room. It could still be heard when she collapsed in Kirall's arms.

"Autumn!" he cried out, slowly lowering her to the floor not understanding what was happening. Changing from her

Dragon form to her Other form shouldn't cause her any pain. Looking at her, he was shocked to see her left leg was at an impossible angle as was her right arm.

Oh Kur! The rods! That's what those metal sounds had been.

They'd put metal rods in for the bones the Varana had crushed. Changing into her Dragon form had forced them from her body. It was how a Dragoon was able to heal from even the most severe of injuries. The power of their Dragon would heal them, but it took time, and Kirall had called her from that form too soon.

"Autumn! Call your Dragon!" he ordered, but she didn't seem to hear him as she continued to scream. Carefully scooping her up into his arms, he turned to Dacke. "Where is the healing unit?!!" he demanded.

"This way." Dacke shoved the remaining human males aside, clearing the corridor so he could lead the way.

"It's going to be alright, Autumn," Kirall murmured, his lips moving against the top of her head. "You're going to be fine. I'm getting you help." Autumn's screams had turned into small, pitiful whimpers the longer he carried her. "Make sure there is a Healer there," he demanded.

"No!" Her single, shaky, pain-filled word had Kirall's stomach clenching, as did the words that followed. "No doctors. No meds. Never again."

"He will only help you, Autumn. It won't be like before, I promise." Reaching the room, he carefully laid her down on the table that housed the healing unit. "Where is the Healer?" he roared over his shoulder.

"He's nearly here," Dacke reassured him, his eyes remaining locked on Autumn.

"Do not look at her!" Kirall spun around, his Beast taking over. "She is mine! My mate!"

135

He gripped Dacke by the throat, pinning him against the far wall as his claws began to draw blood.

"I know that!" Dacke croaked out, lowering his eyes to the more powerful Dragoon. "I meant no challenge. I have just never seen a Supreme before!"

∞ ∞ ∞ ∞ ∞

Bonn slipped into the room unnoticed while Kirall and Dacke fought. Moving to the healing unit, he glared down at the woman who was threatening his livelihood.

First, she misrepresented herself, getting through his security making the aliens question his ability to serve them. Then she didn't take the bolus. If the aliens found out she hadn't taken it, that would be it; and they would find out, when Talfrin wasn't able to alter her memories.

He couldn't let that happen. He wasn't going to let some stupid woman ruin the lifestyle he'd been able to achieve by supplying women to the aliens. He hadn't been sure how he was going to do it, but the aliens had just given him the opportunity, what with the injuries that had been inflicted on her.

Seeing the pressure syringe sitting at the head of the table, the one he knew Talfrin used on the girls to alter their memories, he picked it up. He knew it would be filled with multiple doses of the drug used to relax them. If he gave it all to her it should be enough to kill her, then he could claim he was only trying to help her, that he didn't know it would kill her. They would all blame the alien, Kirall, who had hurt her.

Smiling down at her, he pressed the syringe against her neck and pulled the trigger, again and again and again.

"No!"

Autumn's desperate cry had Kirall spinning around to see Bonn pressing a syringe against his mate's neck.

"What are you doing?!!" Kirall sunk his claws into Bonn's back, ignoring the male's scream as he threw him away from his mate. "Autumn!"

Looking down into her eyes, he saw more than pain. He saw defeat.

"Autumn..." he repeated desperately.

"I can't," she whispered, tears filling her eyes. "I can't go through this again, Kirall. I can't go back to that hell. I won't survive it again." She felt the cold emptiness start to fill her body. The way it had before, only it was stronger this time, more deadly.

"You can!" Kirall argued back. "You are strong."

"I'm not," she told him, wishing she could experience his kiss one last time. But her lips were already numb, and she knew these would be the last words she'd ever say to him.

"I love you," she whispered, and darkness consumed her.

"No!" Kirall roared.

"What is going on?!!" Healer Talfrin demanded as he stormed into the room. He took in the crumbled body of the curator, Dacke's bleeding throat, and the broken female on his table. Had Kirall's Heat driven him mad?

"What have you done to her?!!" he demanded angrily.

"Nothing! The Varana attacked her years ago. Human Healers put metal rods in her arm and leg to replace the crushed bones. When she changed into her Dragon, her body rejected the repairs. I called her from her Dragon form before the injuries were fully healed," Kirall told him in a tortured voice.

"She is Dragoon?" Talfrin stared at the small female in shock. "She survived a Varana attack?"

"Yes, at the age of ten," Kirall told him, "and she is my mate."

"Then why would you give her this?" Talfrin picked up the empty syringe, shaking it at him.

"I didn't!" Kirall instantly denied. "Bonn did!"

"Bonn?!!" Talfrin turned back to the dead curator and spit at him, thinking his death had been too quick.

"Help her!" Kirall demanded.

"I cannot," Talfrin told him regretfully.

"What do you mean?" Kirall's Beast growled angrily.

"She is Dragoon. This amount of drug would render even you immobile. As small as she is... the chances of her surviving are slim."

"NO!" All three parts of him roared, as Kirall's knees slammed into the floor, not feeling the pain as the tile cracked. His head dropped to rest beside his mate.

Talfrin took a startled step back from the naked Prime. The waves of pain pouring off of Kirall were staggering. He had heard about the connection between a male Dragoon and his mate, but had never witnessed it for himself. Kirall helped save his people, his planet. He had to at least try to help him save his mate.

"There might be one way... but she is so young," he said hesitantly.

Kirall raised his head, his Dragon's eyes piercing Talfrin's. "How?" he growled.

∞ ∞ ∞ ∞ ∞

Autumn felt herself sinking deeper and deeper into that dark hell where only pain existed. For a moment, for just the briefest of moments, she had found happiness, acceptance, and love. She knew that was what she'd seen in Kirall's eyes when he'd looked down at her, ready to make love to her again. Then it was ripped away from her, just like her family had been.

As another wave of pain wracked her body, she tried to scream. If she screamed, she knew Kirall would hear her and help. Kirall... was he even real? He'd promised there would be no drugs, but he let Bonn give them to her. Maybe he was just a figment of her imagination, and they had finally broken her.

Maybe she was still in that hospital where they liked to poke and prod her. Where they talked about her like she wasn't even in the room. Maybe they were right, and she really was crazy.

She couldn't turn into a Dragon. Kirall couldn't exist. He had to be a figment of her imagination, and that thought crushed her.

It was time to give up, time to join her family. Then maybe she would find some peace.

∞ ∞ ∞ ∞ ∞

"How?!!" Kirall demanded, his eyes piercing Talfrin's.

"If her Dragon will respond to the call of yours, and if it is strong enough, it should be able to burn the drug out of her system. Then we can worry about the injuries caused by the Varana."

"She will respond to me," Kirall told him confidently rising to his feet. "She is my mate." Kirall didn't even have to think about calling his Dragon, for he was already rising inside Kirall calling out to their mate.

# Chapter Ten

Autumn wasn't finding the peace she thought she would by finally giving up. Instead, her dark world was filled with a deep, rough, coughing sound. It irritated her because it made her want to fight, and fighting only caused more pain.

*"Autumn..."* it called. *"Come back to me. Don't leave me."*

*"Leave me alone,"* she screamed into the darkness. *"I don't know you."*

*"You do know me!"* Slowly the figure of a Dragon began to emerge from the darkness that filled her world, a Dragon with crystalline eyes. *"I am your mate. You are mine,"* it told her. *"You will obey me!"*

*"Mate? Right!"* Something inside her had her hissing at him, challenging him. *"I have no mate! I would not be here if I did. All those I loved, and who loved me, are dead!"*

*"I am not dead! But if death is what you wish then I shall follow you there."*

*"What?"* That brought her up short.

*"I will not live without you now that I have found you. So it will be your choice whether I live or die."*

*"No! No!"* she screamed even knowing no one could hear her. *"No one else dies because of me!"*

*"Then fight!"* he demanded. *"Fight for me, my mate!"*

*"I don't know how!"* she screamed.

*"Let your Dragon out, Autumn. She will guide you. She can use her fire to burn away the drug that is hurting you."*

*"But it will hurt her too!"*

*"For a moment, yes,"* he admitted. *"But she is strong. She is Dragoon and even though she is young, she will know how to protect you, as she has always done. Then we can heal you. I promise you this."*

140

*"You promised that before and it was untrue."* She could feel the pain her words caused him, and what was inside her howled in rage.

*"It was,"* he admitted contritely. *"I should have been more vigilant with you. You are the only thing that matters to me and I failed you, not once but twice. I should have remembered your words. Should have realized your Dragon needed more time to heal the injuries caused by the Varanas. None of this would have happened had I not been an arrogant male that believed himself more than you. Please. Please, do not punish yourself for my mistakes."*

She could hear the honest plea in his voice. Could hear the need. But could she believe it was real? Or was this all in her mind?

A growl came from deep inside her. *"You know I am real, so is our mate,"* it told her. *"Ever since I first emerged you have held me deep inside, and have protected me. Now you need to let me protect you. I can do this. If you let me."*

Autumn had no more than nodded her head when she was engulfed in flames, and all she could do was scream... and scream... and scream... then everything disappeared.

∞ ∞ ∞ ∞ ∞

Autumn's body arched up off the table, stunning everyone as her tortured scream filled the room. She partially shifted, the claws from her good arm extending to slash out blindly at Kirall, the healing unit, and at herself. Anything she could reach.

Kirall paled, wondering what he had done to his mate? "Talfrin!" he begged, even as his eyes remained locked on his mate.

"I can do nothing that will not cause her more pain. Not until the drug is out of her system. I'm sorry. This is a fight she must win on her own."

Kirall crawled up onto the healing bed, lying across her upper body, holding her as gently as he could so she wouldn't harm herself more.

"Please, Autumn," he pleaded, resting his forehead against hers. He could feel how high her temperature had become, and knew it was her Dragon trying to burn the drug out of her system. He just didn't know if she could survive it.

"Please fight, my love," he whispered, not caring if other males heard him begging. "Just a little longer. I am here, fighting with you. Feel my strength. Take what you need. Take all of it, if that is what you need for I am nothing without you." He captured her lips with his own, and breathed his life into her.

As suddenly as it started, Autumn went completely still, her claws retracting and her body cooling.

∞ ∞ ∞ ∞ ∞

Talfrin put a hand on Kirall's shoulder. "You need to let me treat her now, Kirall."

"No! I won't leave her!" He couldn't.

"The unit can't heal her with you covering her like that."

"What?" Kirall gave him a confused look.

"Your mate's Dragon is strong, Kirall. It was able to burn the drug out of her system. Now let me heal the rest, starting with her arm."

Kirall reluctantly rose, giving Talfrin and the machine the room they needed to heal his mate, but he kept a hand on her, reassuring himself that she was alive.

Talfrin harrumphed his displeasure that Kirall wouldn't move completely out of his way, but his fingers still activated the healing unit. "Dacke," he called out. "Make yourself useful. Get me a blanket for her, and some pants for Kirall. Both are in the cabinet behind you."

"I'm fine," Kirall growled. "And my mate's name is Autumn."

"I'll remember that, but I have no desire to see any more of your cock than I already have."

"Here." Dacke slapped the pants against Kirall's chest then held out the blanket to Talfrin.

"I'll do it," Kirall said, ignoring the pants thrust at him as he reached for the blanket. "She is mine to care for."

"Cover everything except the arm I'm working on," Talfrin ordered, closely watching how the machine healed Autumn. "And for the love of Kur, put your pants on!"

Kirall stepped into the pants, keeping a hand on Autumn. They were too short for him, but at least they had a self-adjusting waistband.

"Her arm has healed nicely, but it would be best if she were on her stomach to heal her leg." Talfrin reached out to roll her, only to stop as Kirall released a deadly growl.

"Do not touch her." Talfrin and Dacke both watched as Kirall struggled to control his Beast and Dragon. Finally, he was able to speak. "I will move her."

Slipping his arms under her, Kirall rolled her over as carefully as he could, praying to Kur he wasn't hurting her. When the blanket slipped away, he heard the shocked hisses from the other two males.

"Praise Kur!" Dacke hissed.

"Who did this to her?!!" Talfrin demanded, taking in her damaged back.

"General Terron," Kirall spat out, covering her back.

143

"Terron!" Both males looked at him in shock.

"Yes. When she was ten, he and two of his soldiers attacked her family, killing all but her. They savaged her because she tried to protect her brother."

"She survived... with all this damage... at ten?" Talfrin asked disbelievingly.

"She is not damaged!" Kirall roared at Talfrin. "Never say that again!"

"I meant no offense, Prime Kirall," Talfrin bowed his head to him. "I only meant to express my respect and awe. I have never heard of a Dragoon so young being able to survive a direct attack by the Varana. They usually remain until they are sure the Dragoon is dead." Talfrin's fingers began to fly over the controls of the healing unit again.

"They only left because Autumn severely injured Terron," Kirall told them.

"What?!!" the shocked word came from both men.

"The scars Terron now carries on his face were caused by my Autumn. She was able to partially shift when she tried to protect her brother."

"She is the one who took his eye?" Dacke asked. "At only ten?"

"Yes."

"Then we owe her a great deal, and will make sure she fully recovers."

"Her scars?" Kirall had to ask.

"No." Talfrin looked at Kirall, true regret filling his gaze. "I'm sorry. Too much time has passed since she was injured. Maybe as she and her Dragon grow the scars might fade, but they will never completely disappear. I'm sorry."

"I am not." Kirall slipped his arms under his mate when the healing unit indicated her leg was healed. "They are a part of

144

my mate. A part of what has made her so strong. I do not want that to ever fade or for us to forget her family.

∞ ∞ ∞ ∞ ∞

Autumn floated in the white nothingness that now surrounded her. She felt so strange. There was no pain, no nightmares, no screams, and no blood. She liked it here, wherever here was.

Was this heaven?

If so, then where was her family?

"This is not heaven," a voice spoke, and the whiteness began to swirl and shift revealing a man, a very tall man who had red hair with silver tips.

"Then where am I?" Autumn asked finding she was standing instead of floating.

"Someplace else. A world between worlds." Brilliant green eyes assessed her. "You truly are very small and young to have achieved so much."

"I have achieved nothing," Autumn argued back.

"You have fought and won against the Varana. You have shifted into your Dragon form, and you have found your mate. There are Dragoons that live their entire existence that never achieve any of those things. You are a true Supreme."

"The Varana won! They killed my family!" she argued back.

"Yes, but not you. They died because they were not able to call their Dragon. You could, so you lived."

"I didn't..."

"You did. You know you did. How else do you think you were able to injure a Varana? With those puny things?" He pointed to her hand, making her look at her short nails. "No.

You did what only a female Supreme can do. You partially shifted. You do me proud, young one."

"Do you 'proud'? What do you mean?"

"You descend from me. From the offspring my mate and I had together eons ago. I feared the power we imbued in them had faded with the passing of time, but I see it is still there."

"If I descend from you then so did the rest of my family."

"Yes."

"So if I shifted like you said then why couldn't they, especially Mom and Dad?"

"Because they didn't feel the power, not as you and your brother did. It is why the Varana didn't find them sooner."

"You're saying it's our fault? Jack's and mine that we were attacked?"

"No!" the man denied. "It is the Varana's. You and Jack were doing nothing more than what was natural for you, as it is for any Dragoon. Had the Varana not threatened you, you may never have shifted. Would have never realized what you truly were. But now you have, and you can never go back to being what you were."

"Which is?"

"Human. You are now a Supreme Dragoon, a very young, but very powerful Supreme Dragoon. Who has taken an inferior mate."

"What do you mean 'inferior'?!! Kirall is the most powerful of all the Primes! He is a Black."

"A paltry being." The man waved a hand dismissively.

"Paltry!" Autumn felt her anger rising, and claws began extending from her fingers. "Who are you to claim that?!!"

"Why I am Razeth. Do you not recognize me?" He gave her a confused look.

A gentle laugh swirled through the mist. It had Autumn's Beast retreating as a beautiful woman stepped from it. She had long, black hair with silver tips.

"You have always been an arrogant one, my love," she said as she smiled, then laughed again seeing his putout look.

"It is not arrogance if it is true," he grumbled at her.

"That is also true, but there is no reason for Autumn to recognize you."

"Blood should always recognize blood."

"True, but have you given her the chance to? How did you think she'd react to your slur against her mate? How would you react if it were against me?"

"I would destroy anyone that spoke against you!" The words were instantaneous and trembled with power.

"Yet you expect less from one of your own?" The woman raised an eyebrow at him.

"No," Razeth huffed out heavily before leaning down to kiss the woman. "As usual, you are right, my love."

"Of course I am."

"And that's not arrogance?" Autumn asked, and found herself the recipient of Razeth's ferocious frown, while the woman only laughed.

"And one of mine. She reminds me a great deal of Adalinda, don't you think?"

"Perhaps," Razeth said, still frowning at Autumn."

"Ignore him, he frowned at our first female that way too."

"First female..." Autumn frowned. "I'm sorry, but just who are you?"

The woman put a hand on Razeth's arm, and he immediately stopped growling. "I'm sorry, Autumn, it seems I've become as arrogant as my mate. I am Jaclyn, Razeth's mate."

"How do you know who I am?" Autumn asked.

"Because you are one of ours." Jaclyn looked up at Razeth. "Blood recognizes blood, at least in the Dragoon world, and it has been a long time since we have heard its call."

"I don't understand," Autumn said.

"She doesn't..." Razeth started in an exasperated tone.

"Stop, Razeth! How can you expect her to understand? Did I when you first claimed me? She is no different than me, even though your blood runs through her veins. There has been no one there to teach her, and she is still very young; only twenty and two. Not even our own offspring understood everything until they were much, much older." Her gaze returned to Autumn. "Let me tell you a story..."

"A long, long time ago, there was a young girl who lived next to a mountain. She was a plain girl."

Razeth gave a rumble of displeasure that had Jaclyn smiling.

"A plain girl," she stressed, "whose father was about to marry her off to the village blacksmith. The girl didn't want to marry the blacksmith, for he was a cruel, older man who had already lost two wives during childbirth. She didn't want to be the third. So she ran away; up into the mountains. She knew it would mean certain death, but she preferred a death of her choosing instead of the one she knew awaited her in the village."

"You were very brave," Autumn told her, and Jaclyn gave her a small smile.

"I was very desperate. I waited for a winter storm to come because I knew no one would follow me out into it. I was half-frozen when Razeth found me." She looked lovingly up into Razeth's face.

"He was so handsome, so strong, so warm. He took me to his lair and made me his."

"Just like that?" Autumn questioned.

"Yes," Razeth said.

"No," Jaclyn said simultaneously.

"You couldn't resist me," Razeth claimed, wrapping his arms around her, pulling her close.

"Your mind is going because you are so old. I fought you and escaped. More than once." Jaclyn's gaze dared him to deny it.

"True, but I always brought you back."

"And I will always be grateful for that." She rose up on her toes, and he lifted her so they could kiss.

As the kiss went on and on, Autumn cleared her throat. "I think I'll just leave you two alone."

"No." Jaclyn pulled her mouth from Razeth's, who had a self-satisfied expression on his face. "Razeth likes to do that to me. Put me down, you big lug."

"Do what?" Autumn asked, watching as Razeth slowly lowered Jaclyn down his body.

"Distract me." Jaclyn gave her mate an exasperated look. "He likes to see how long it takes."

"Does it ever take long?" Autumn asked.

"No." Jaclyn gave her a knowing grin. "And it won't for you with your mate either. Which brings us back to my story. I willingly stayed with my Dragoon. Willingly mated with him. We had many offspring and a wonderful life for more years than I can remember."

"What happened?" Autumn wasn't sure she wanted to know.

"Varana…" Jaclyn whispered, and felt Razeth's arms tighten around her. "They attacked while Razeth was out teaching our young. They had never appeared on Earth before, and while Razeth had prepared protections, I had wandered out past them. There was no chance for Razeth to get to me in time. I am not like you, Autumn, even with Razeth's blood running through me. I am unable to shift, so I was unable to defend myself."

"I didn't either," Autumn denied.

"You did," Jaclyn argued back. "You wouldn't be here if you hadn't been able to. You may not have won, but you survived to fight another day, and that is more than I was able to do."

"You died?" Autumn asked quietly.

"Yes, and because I did, so did my mate." She looked sadly up at Razeth. "Our offspring were left to fend for themselves, and for many centuries they were able to. But over time, fewer and fewer of their offspring were able to call their Dragon form, forgetting where they came from until now, only you remain."

"Only me?" Autumn whispered.

"Yes. You, Autumn, are the last of our line on Earth."

"That's why…"

"You were attacked so viciously, yes," Jaclyn told her. "With your death, the Varana would have finally been able to eradicate the Supremes. Instead, you survived."

"Barely."

"That matters not. What matters is that you did, and now you have a mate who can protect you while you grow. He will teach you what you need to know, the way mine taught me."

"Not if he can't protect her!" Razeth argued.

"Kirall does protect me!" Autumn took an angry step toward Razeth.

"Not very well," Razeth told her even though he was secretly proud she would challenge him. She truly was one of theirs, "and not if he remains a Prime."

"What are you talking about?" Autumn demanded.

"Your mate has bonded with *you*. It is *your* choice whether to bond with him... or not," Razeth told her.

"What are you talking about? And his name is Kirall!"

"Autumn," Jaclyn said, quietly pulling her attention back to her. "You are a Supreme. The very last one. Kirall is a Prime. For him to truly become your mate, you must give him *your* kiss and *your* blood. He will then become the first male Supreme on Mondu since Razeth left. Together, you will rebuild the Dragoon world, and have the chance to finally defeat the Varana."

"I..."

"He is a... worthy Dragoon," Razeth grudgingly told her. "Maybe not worthy enough for one of mine..."

"Ours," Jaclyn reminded him, "and if he is her choice, then you must accept and support it."

"If I must," he agreed reluctantly looking from his mate to Autumn. "My power will recognize you once you arrive on Mondu. It would please me greatly if you and your mate... Kirall... were to reside in Kruba."

Autumn's eyes widened, "Kirall said it is in the highest and most coveted mountain range on the entire planet. That no one has been able to live there since you left."

Razeth's chest seemed to puff up at her words. "This is true, but *you* will be able to. Because you are ours. Now it is time for us to return to our world, and for you to return to yours."

## Chapter Eleven

Autumn opened her eyes, and found she was in a dimly lit room staring up at a ceiling she'd never seen before. Where was she? Slowly, her senses began to kick in. She could hear a low hum. It sounded mechanical, but it wasn't from any machine she recognized. She was lying on something flat, but it was comfortable. There was something soft covering her body, and something warm was wrapped around her waist. She felt safe and protected. Taking a cautious breath, she smelled... Kirall.

Turning her head to the side, she found his face inches from hers, and while he was asleep, there were still lines of stress and fatigue on his face. They didn't belong there. Glancing down, she realized it was his arm around her waist that was making her feel so warm and protected. Looking up, she found his eyes were open, his gaze piercing hers.

She watched him slowly blink, his gaze quickly moving over her face as if he couldn't believe she was there.

"You're finally awake," he said, his voice a little ragged.

"I am." Autumn frowned at his words. "How long have I been out?"

"Three days." Kirall rose up on an elbow, his eyes full of concern. "How are you feeling?"

Autumn didn't immediately answer, taking time to really think about how she felt. The ache she'd always felt in her damaged arm and leg was no longer there. And the feeling she'd always had that there was something deep inside her, trying to get out, was gone too.

*"That is because you have finally accepted me,"* the voice she recognized as her Dragon said.

*"I'm sorry it has taken me so long,"* she answered.

*"It is how it needed to be, so we could survive and find our mate."*

"Autumn?" Kirall's question brought her back from her internal conversation.

"Good. I feel good," she told him.

"You're sure?"

"Yes, I haven't felt this good since before the Varana attacked me." She raised a hand to gently cup his cheek. "Why do you look so tired? So worried?"

Kirall frowned, "You don't remember what happened?"

"I remember someone bursting into our room, and you went out to confront them. Alone." She gave him a look that told him she wasn't happy about that. "I wasn't going to let you do that. I wasn't going to fail someone else I loved, so I... shifted." Her eyes widened. She'd actually shifted.

"You did." He smiled, running a gentle finger along her jaw. "Into the most beautiful Dragon I have ever seen."

"Really?" she asked, looking up at him uncertainly.

"You were beautiful, Autumn. *Are* beautiful, never doubt that." Leaning down, he rested his forehead against hers. "I am so sorry, Autumn."

"For what?" she asked, caressing the back of his neck, not understanding.

"For not truly listening to you." He pulled back slightly and forced himself to meet her gaze. "You told me how the Varana had injured you. What the Earth Healers had done to repair the damage, and still I called you from your Dragon form."

"So?"

"So when you shifted into your Dragon, your Dragon expelled the foreign substances from your body. It is how a Dragon repairs any injuries you might receive in your Other form."

"I still don't understand what you are sorry about." She lifted her arm. Looking at it, the scar was still there, but the ache was gone. "It feels wonderful. She did a good job."

"Your Dragon didn't repair you, Autumn." He looked down at her, his eyes full of regret. "As I said, I called you from your Dragon form too soon."

"Then how?"

"You collapsed in my arms screaming." Kirall shuddered slightly, remembering. He never wanted to hear her scream like that again. "I tried to call your Dragon back, but I couldn't, so I rushed you to the healing unit."

"I... something happened there... " Her delicate eyebrows drew closer together, then she whispered. "Bonn..."

"Yes," Kirall gave her a guilt-ridden look. "After I laid you on the healing unit, I turned to confront Dacke. Bonn entered without me noticing, and was able to inject you with multiple doses of the drug used to relax the females, before I could stop him."

"He had this look on his face, of enjoyment," she whispered. "It reminded me of the Varana. He knew what he was doing was going to hurt me, and it did... so much," she whispered. "It was like the drug they gave me in the hospital. It pulled me back into that dark world of pain and immobility."

"I would have willingly given my entire hoard if I could have prevented you from going through that, Autumn."

"I know." She gently cupped his cheek. "What did you do... to Bonn?"

"I killed him," he told her bluntly.

Autumn was shocked to discover she was nodding understandingly, then realized it was what she would have done if someone had harmed Kirall.

154

"But Talfrin couldn't heal you while the drug was still in your system."

"Then how?" she asked.

"I had to call on your Dragon. She was weakened, but able to burn the drug out of your system."

"I heard you..." she whispered. "In my head, you were pleading with me to not give up. That you would join me in death if that was where I was going."

"I would follow you anywhere, for I will never be separated from you now that I have found you."

"Even into the white world between worlds?" she asked.

"Even there," he instantly replied, then gave her a stunned look. "How do you know about that place?"

"Because I was there after the darkness let me go. I met Razeth and his mate there." She watched Kirall's mouth drop open.

"You met Razeth...?"

"Yes, and he is a very arrogant male, much like someone else I know," she raised an eyebrow at him, letting him know who she was referring to.

"Are you saying that I am arrogant?" His eyebrow matched hers.

"Of course you are, you are a Black Prime, the strongest of the strong, the most powerful of all the Dragoons."

"Not anymore." His eyebrow lowered as did his voice. "Now, *you* are the most powerful."

"Right," she said sarcastically. "Just because I am a Supreme, it doesn't mean that I'm the most powerful."

"It does in the Dragoon world," he told her.

"Kirall..."

"Autumn, you do not understand how truly rare and special you are. You are only twenty-two, and yet you can already shift

155

into your full Dragon form. No other Dragoon is able to do that before they are fifty. At ten, you were able to partially shift. There are male Dragoons that have never mastered that skill, and I have never heard of a female doing it."

"Razeth said it is something only female Supremes can do."

"And you don't see yourself as special?" Kirall gave her a disbelieving look. "You also severely injured a Varana, their strongest one, all by yourself. Your strength and skills will only grow with time. Before you know it, you will even surpass me."

"But I don't want to surpass you," she denied. "I just want to be with you, to be your mate, and share my life with you."

"Autumn." He lowered his forehead to hers again. He had thought long and hard about this over the last three days. He had thought he had made her *his* mate when he'd given her his kiss and shared his blood with her; that he had bonded her to him, but he hadn't. *She* was a *Supreme*, the more powerful Dragoon. She had to claim him as *her* mate for the bond to truly form. "There is nothing I want more than to be with you. But I have made so many mistakes that I would not fault you for looking for another." He raised his head slightly. "It is what a Prime female would do if the male she was considering had failed her so badly."

"Then it's lucky for you that I'm not a Prime, isn't it?" Her hand tugged hard on his hair. "And you haven't failed me! I'm not perfect, Kirall. My scars prove that. Quiet!" she ordered sharply when he growled his displeasure at her words. "I'm just me. Autumn. The same girl that came to your room a few days ago. The same girl that irritated and angered you. The same girl that trusted you enough to reveal what she's never revealed to anyone else. The one that you said was your mate. Has that changed for you now that you know I am a Supreme?"

"No! Kur, Autumn... but I just want you to know you have options. My Dragon is shredding my insides, and my Beast is ready to beat me to a bloody pulp for telling you, but I refuse to lie to you."

"Stop," she whispered, putting a hand on his chest and Kirall felt both his Beast and Dragon calm. "I know you would never lie to me, Kirall." She saw the relief in his eyes.

The steady hum she'd been hearing changed for a moment then settled back to how it was.

"What was that?" she asked.

"It's just the engines of the Inferno. They are adjusting our course for Mondu," he told her.

"Wait. What? The Inferno? Mondu?" Sitting up, she realized she was wearing some type of nightgown. It was strapless and had something built into it that held it just above her breasts. It felt soft and silky against her skin. She looked to Kirall who had also sat up.

"Talfrin offered this to me after he healed you. He has been studying Earth females and thought you would like to have something to wear." He ran a finger along the upper swell of her breasts. "I would prefer you without it."

"I can't be naked all the time, Kirall," she told him laughing.

"Why not?" he growled as she pulled his finger away.

"Because I can't. At least not right now," she teased. "Now. The Inferno and Mondu. Tell me."

"The Inferno is the ship that brought us to Earth, and that is now taking us home."

"Home..." she frowned

"Yes. Home. Our home," he repeated, "in the Papier mountains on Mondu."

"Don't you think you should have asked me first?" She pulled slightly away from him.

"Asked?" Kirall gave her a confused look.

"Yes, Mister 'Are you saying that I am arrogant?' Dragoon." She air quoted with her fingers. "Asked. Maybe I don't want to live on Mondu. Maybe you should be the one that has to move."

"Me? Move to Earth?" Kirall looked at her in utter shock. "Where would we live? How would I protect you? It's not as if you have any family left there. On Mondu, I have family, and they can help me protect you."

He watched Autumn's eyes flash silver before her face went completely blank, and she shoved her way past him getting up off the bed. He gave her a confused look, then realized what he had said.

"Autumn…" he gave her a contrite look.

"Is that the bathroom?" She pointed to the door where it had been in their other rooms.

"Yes," he told her.

"Then I'm going to take a shower." With that, she left him alone.

Kirall fell back on the bed, thumping a hard fist against his forehead. How could he be such a stupid male?!! Was he *trying* to drive her away? He knew how she felt about her family. How she felt she had failed them. She hadn't, but he didn't think he'd ever get her to believe that, no matter how long they lived.

She was right. He was an arrogant male. He was used to being able to say and do whatever he wanted, to whomever he wanted, and he never worried about how it affected them. He couldn't do that with Autumn because what affected her, affected him. He needed to explain to her that he now understood that.

Rising, he went to tell her.

∞ ∞ ∞ ∞ ∞

Autumn entered the room and found it was nothing like the one on Earth. First of all it was smaller, probably a necessary thing when you were traveling in outer space where 'space' was at a premium. There was something small and reflective on a wall, but she ignored it. She really didn't care how she looked. There was something that stuck out of the wall that she assumed was a toilet along with an enclosed space that she discovered was a shower stall when she looked in.

Pulling the nightgown over her head, she was about to drop it when she remembered Kirall's words. This man called Talfrin had not only healed her, but had been considerate enough to think of her needs. She wasn't going to repay that kindness by mistreating what he had provided.

Carefully, she folded the delicate garment and set it on the narrow counter. Turning, she stepped into the shower stall then just stared at what she found.

∞ ∞ ∞ ∞ ∞

"Push the darker tile on your right," Kirall told her and saw her stiffen when she heard his words. He'd entered the cleansing room, surprised the shower wasn't running. He stripped off his sleeping pants before following her into the unit. Seeing her staring at the wall had him realizing why. She didn't know how to work the unit.

Autumn pushed and held the dark tile, and suddenly hot water was streaming into her face. Crying out, she jumped back bumping into Kirall.

Kirall immediately wrapped his arms around her, turning so his back took the brunt of the heat as his arm reached behind him to adjust the temperature.

"I'm sorry," he whispered into her hair. "I should have told you that the longer you hold it the hotter it gets. There's a great deal I'm sorry for, my Aud-um."

Slowly she turned in his arms, gripping the bulging biceps as she looked at him, his broad shoulders blocking the spray.

"Haven't I already told you that if you're going to enter someone's shower uninvited that you should at least know how to say their name?" She repeated the words she'd told him that first day she'd met him, but this time there was no heat in them.

"I know your name, Autumn, but you will always be 'Aud-um' to me, because you are so precious to me."

"Am I?" she questioned.

"Yes, of course!" Carefully he gripped her waist, lifting her so they were eye-to-eye. "Have I not shown you that? Do you doubt my commitment to you?"

"No." She wrapped her legs around his waist. "I don't doubt your commitment to me, Kirall, but I think you doubt mine to you." She saw by the flare in his eyes that she was right. Suddenly she remembered something he said earlier. "You still think I would choose another. Someone like Dacke. That is why you were 'distracted' by him."

"Yes," Kirall growled, his hands sliding to her hips, holding her firmly against him.

"Why would you think that? I don't know this Dacke. Have never even met him. He has been with Kristy, while I have only ever been with you. You told me how he bragged about being with Kristy to anyone that would listen. He could walk in here right now, and I wouldn't know who he was."

"He'd better not come in here if he wants to live," his Beast growled. "He's already seen you naked once. I will kill him if he ever sees you that way again."

"So that's what distracted you? Him, seeing me naked?" She couldn't believe it.

"That, and he looked at you with interest," he admitted.

"I can't believe he could have found anything very 'interesting' with the condition I was in."

"He saw you in your Dragon form, and realized you were a Supreme."

"So it wasn't really me he was interested in, but what I was."

"Yes."

"Well now, that just pisses me off."

Kirall watched the silver flash in her eyes, and his own anger faded away. He could almost feel sorry for Dacke when he and Autumn did finally meet. She was going to burn him. Kirall couldn't wait to see it, but right now he needed to make sure she didn't burn *him*.

"I am sorry for my earlier words about your family, Autumn. It was not my intent to upset you. It seems that I *am* that arrogant male you accused me of being. I never once considered that you might not want to travel to Mondu, might not want to make my home, your home."

"That's because you are a Black Prime, and are used to getting your way." She slowly ran her hands up his arms, bringing them to rest on either side of his neck.

"This is true," he agreed.

"Is it going to upset you when you're not?"

"Not what?" he asked. "Arrogant?"

"I have no doubt that you will always be arrogant, Kirall, and while it can be irritating," she gave him a teasing smile, "I can't imagine you any other way." Leaning forward she caught his lower lip between her teeth.

"Then what?" His words were distracted as she continued to nibble on his lip. His hands tightened on her hips as his cock started to harden.

"You, not being a Black Prime anymore. Once I claim you."

"What?!!!" He jerked his lip from her teeth, staring at her in shock.

"It's going to take some getting used to." She sank her fingers into his silky strands. "You not having all this beautiful black hair. I'll miss it."

Kirall couldn't believe she was concerned about the color of his hair. "I don't care about the color of my hair, Autumn, and would willingly cut it all off, if it meant I was yours."

"You're sure?" She gave him a small smile as she tightened her legs around his waist, pulling herself up slightly so her nipples teased his chest. She'd felt his cock start to harden when she nibbled on his lip, and it was continuing to grow. "I would hate for you to do something you weren't... up for."

"You think I'm not... up... for being your mate?" he growled at her challenge, rocking his hips up, his cock bumping the entrance of her lair.

"You'd better be," she found herself growling back, as a sudden hunger filled her. It rose from the deepest parts of her soul, burning stronger and hotter as it sought release. Instinctively she knew it was her very essence wanting to be shared with her mate, to begin the claiming process.

Using the fingers still in his hair, she pulled his mouth back to hers, capturing it for a hard hot kiss, giving all she was to her mate.

Kirall just caught the flash of Autumn's Dragon in her eyes before he was engulfed in the heat of her kiss.

His Dragon roared his pleasure as the claws of his Beast extended, digging into her hips, pulling her down as he thrust up embedding himself inside her in one hard stroke.

Never in his life had he experienced a Heat like this. It burned through him. It was painful. It felt amazing. It consumed all that he was before while preparing him for what was to come.

"Autumn!" he ripped his mouth from hers, pressing her shoulders back against the stall wall, thrusting harder and deeper into her again and again. Seeing his mating mark at the base of her neck drove him even higher, and he lowered his head, latching onto it.

"Kirall!" Autumn's head fell back as pleasure flooded her system. Her channel clenched around his cock with each tug of his mouth, driving her need higher as her mate loved her. No, not her mate. Not yet. And that was unacceptable to every part of her.

Her eyes that had closed from the pleasure he was giving her, shot open at that thought, and zeroed in on the juncture of his neck and shoulder. Her eyes elongated, turning silver as her Dragon rose, taking over. Another stronger wave of heat rose up in her and she struck, driven by an instinct older than time, her teeth sinking deep into the soft, giving flesh.

Kirall reared back, his roar cut off as his entire body seized as Autumn took his blood, mixed it with her own more powerful Supreme blood, then injected it back into him. It blasted through his system incinerating everything he knew he was, everything he thought he was, until the only thing left was ash. His legs that had never let him down began to shake, and his vision started to dim. For a moment he thought he would be meeting Kur, then just as he was about to collapse, something started to stir in the ashes.

It slowly swirled and pulsed, picking up speed as it gathered up his remains. Suddenly it burst forth with new life, burning Kirall in the flames of his rebirth. Legs that had been about to give out were now stronger than they'd ever been. The chest that had been starved for the life-giving air, sucked in a deep breath, expanding and growing larger than before. His eyes began to refocus, then flashed silver when he found his mate watching him.

"Mine," he growled, feeling an overwhelming heat of possession and desire flooding him, and he began pounding into her with a cock bigger, harder, and hotter than it had been before.

"Mine," she challenged back, pulling his mouth to hers, consuming it as she matched him thrust for thrust.

As they touched, kissed and loved, a final wave of heat flowed over them causing them to explode together in ecstasy. It created the first mated pair of Supremes the Universe had seen in thousands of years.

# Epilogue

Autumn opened her eyes, and while she recognized the room from before, this time she was alone in the bed. Sitting up, the blankets covering her fell away. Unconcerned with her nakedness, she rose from the bed and went looking for her mate.

She found him in the bathroom, staring at his image in what was now a large reflective mirror. His black hair now only ran part way down its length before it became red. It reminded her of the flames from their family bonfires that used to shoot up high into the dark, summer skies. His fingers were rubbing his now silver laminae.

But that wasn't the only thing about him that had changed, only the most obvious. You had to look closely to notice the other changes. His biceps were a little bigger. His back a little broader. And there was an aura of power surrounding him that was undeniable.

"Does it bother you?" she asked quietly, watching him carefully.

Kirall's eyes captured hers in the mirror, and she was surprised to see they had changed too. They were rimmed with silver now.

"No." He turned away from the mirror and leaned against the counter to look at her. "It pleases me greatly. I can't express to you how it makes me feel to know that when others look at me now, they will know that you chose me to be your mate. I especially like that my eyes are the same as yours."

"Like mine?" She gave him a confused look.

It was only then that Kirall realized Autumn hadn't noticed the changes that she had gone through. Pushing away from the counter, he gently gripped her arms, then turned, so they both faced the mirror. He saw her eyes widen when she noticed the silver that now rimmed her eyes, and understood her amazement as she touched her now silver laminae.

"You are so beautiful, my mate," his voice rumbled deeper than before.

"I hadn't realized..." She continued to rub her hair, her eyes locking with his in the mirror. "I don't really feel any different except that I can now feel my Dragon. I'm not bigger or stronger like you are."

"That is because you have always been stronger than me, Autumn. You just didn't know it."

"No..."

"Yes!" The hands gripping her arms tightened. "Look at yourself, Autumn. You are a Supreme. The strongest of the strong."

"But you are so much bigger than me, Kirall. Stronger." For some reason, tears started to flow down her cheeks.

Kirall turned her toward him, his thumbs wiping away her tears. "That's because you are only twenty-two. I am a great deal older than you, Autumn."

"So are you telling me I mated an old man?" She gave him a weak smile, and enjoyed his rumble of displeasure then let out a squeal when he lifted her onto the counter.

"Male!" he corrected. "And I will show you just how 'old' I am," he told her moving between her thighs, his cock sliding along her clit as he leaned down to kiss her.

Autumn let herself sink into the kiss, savoring Kirall's spicy flavor. This was her mate. She was finally home.

"I can't wait to get you to our home on Mondu," he murmured against her lips. "I will teach you everything my parents taught me. I will show you how to call your Dragon;

how to control your fire; and how to spread your wings and fly on the updrafts surrounding my home."

"Why can't you teach me now?" she asked, pouting slightly as she looked up at him.

"Do you remember what I told you about my younger brother, Zeb?" he asked, fighting the need to just give into her.

"You mean about him torching your sister's hair?"

"Yes. We are in space, Autumn. Uncontrolled Dragon fire does not work so well out here."

"Oh, I see." She gave him a hesitant look.

"What?" he asked, seeing she had something she wanted to say.

"Would you be very upset if we didn't live in your home in the Papier Mountains?" She bit her upper lip as she waited for his answer.

"I... What???" Kirall frowned. "But if not there, then where?"

"How would you feel about living in Kruba?"

"Kruba?!!"

"Yes. Razeth asked that we live there, that his power would recognize me and welcome us."

"It would," Kirall agreed. "I just never considered... Kruba..."

"So it would be okay if we lived there?"

"It would, my little Aud-um." Kirall repositioned her on the counter. "Although we may need to set up special protections so members of my family don't just show up."

"I would love for your family to do that," she told him, wrapping her legs around his hips.

"Really... because I plan on keeping you naked and loving you in every room of Kruba for at least the next hundred years." His cock nudged the entrance to her lair.

"Oh," she gasped, desire filling her. "Well, I see what you mean. We can't have them interrupting us all the time." And with that she let her mate love her.

∞ ∞ ∞ ∞ ∞

Michelle has always loved to read and writing is just a natural extension of this for her. Growing up, she always loved to extend the stories of books she'd read just to see where the characters went. Happily married for over twenty five years she is the proud mother of two grown children and with the house empty has found time to write again. You can reach her at m.k.eidem@live.com        or        her        website        at http://www.mkeidem.com she'd love to hear your comments.

∞ ∞ ∞ ∞ ∞

Printed in Great Britain
by Amazon